Imogen: A Pastoral Romance

Edwin (and) Imogen.

IMOGEN

A Pastoral Romance

From the Ancient British

By WILLIAM GODWIN

Reprinted from the 1784 Edition

With an Introduction by JACK W. MARKEN and
Critical Discussion by MARTHA WINBURN ENGLAND,
BURTON R. POLLIN, and IRWIN PRIMER

New York
The New York Public Library
1 9 6 3

Library of Congress Catalog Card Number: 63–18142

Reprinted from the
Bulletin of The New York Public Library
January – June 1963
form p714 [viii-20-63 1m]

Foreword

*T*HIS *volume comprises the first modern publication of William Godwin's "Pastoral Romance" — lost to the world since its original publication in 1784 — plus the first comments of literary historians upon it. The combination is meant to repair a small but significant gap in the history of the English novel that has lain open for almost two centuries.*

The text is transcribed from the copy recently discovered by Professor Marken and now in the Berg Collection. Two lacking leaves were supplied, in photocopy, from the only other copy known, by the courtesy of the Salisbury Library. The frontispiece is reproduced from the original work, but we have taken the liberty of supplying ornaments between chapters from the pastoral wood-cuts of William Blake, who was acquainted with Godwin if not with Imogen. *These Blake cuts are reproduced from a copy in the Prints Division of the work in which they first appeared, the third edition (1821) of Thornton's* The Pastorals of Virgil.

Table of Contents

BOOK the SIXTH

APPENDIX: CRITICAL DISCUSSION

Introduction

WILLIAM GODWIN is known as the author of two important eighteenth century works, the *Enquiry Concerning Political Justice*, 1793, and *Caleb Williams*, 1794; but few know about his various writings before he achieved a permanent fame with these books. No other period of his life was so full of publications as the dozen years preceding *Political Justice*. Beginning with his biography of William Pitt the elder, finished in 1782, and including several political pamphlets, writings for three journals, besides such miscellaneous pamphlets as a prospectus for establishing a seminary for teaching young men and a review of works not yet published, the period was called by Godwin "probably the busiest" of his life, and he summarized it thus: ". . . in the latter end of 1783, I wrote in ten days a novel, entitled Damon and Delia, for which Hookham gave me five guineas, and a novel in three weeks, called Italian Letters, purchased by Robinson for twenty guineas, and in the first four months of 1784 a novel called Imogen, a Pastoral Romance, for which Lane gave me ten pounds." [1]

Most of his early works can be found in libraries, but, as Godwin's biographers have pointed out, the early novels have vanished into nothingness. The only information we have about the two earliest novels is supplied by the contemporary reviews, by Mary Shelley in the fragments of an unpublished biography of her father, and by Godwin himself. We find that *Damon and Delia* has a Mr Godfrey as a main character. He is, as Mary Shelley points out, Godwin himself.[2] We know that *Italian Letters* is Godwin's only experiment in the epistolary form, and we can find excerpts from it in the *Critical Review*, LXVIII (Sept 1784) 211–213. But fortunately, for a fuller

---

[1] Quoted from the Godwin papers in Lord Abinger's possession. Godwin lists these works in chronological order, but in a letter dated Feb 5 1796 Miss Amelia Alderson (later Mrs Opie) wrote to him: "I called on your old friend Mrs. Southern about a month ago, and asked her opinion of 'Caleb Williams:' Now, pray let not thy noble courage be cast down when I inform you that both Mrs S. and her daughter think you talk too favourably of wicked men, and that 'Italian Letters' (your first novel), are vastly prettier than 'Caleb Williams.'" See C. Kegan Paul, *William Godwin: His Friends and Contemporaries* (Boston 1876) I 158. The payment Godwin received for his early novels was usual for the times. Joyce M. S. Tompkins, *The Popular Novel in England, 1770–1800* (rept, University of Nebraska Press 1961) p 9, says: "The usual payment for a library novel seems to have been between five and ten guineas, and the profit could be doubled by a judicious dedication. Sometimes the bookseller gave as much as twenty guineas. . . ."

[2] Unfortunately, the contemporary reviews give little information about the plot of this novel. The reviews indicate that Mr Godfrey is more important than Damon and Delia. Their names suggest that Godwin is already thinking about the pastoral.

knowledge of Godwin, two copies of *Imogen: A Pastoral Romance* have been found. The only complete copy is in the Salisbury Library of the University College of South Wales and Monmouth. The other copy, which lacks two leaves, pages 131–134, in Volume 2, is now in the Berg Collection of The New York Public Library.

This small two-volume novel was published by William Lane in 1784.[3] With the exception of his biography of William Pitt, which went through two editions and was pirated in Dublin, this novel was evidently Godwin's most ambitious project. He took longer to write it than any other early work, and it served as a kind of model for his later novels.

Like most of them, it contains a frontispiece and a preface. The frontispiece is an engraving intended to convey the mood of the pastoral. The scene is a valley in which, like Daphnis and Chloe, the young lovers are together. Imogen sits in a bed of flowers in front of three tall oak trees near a meandering stream. Edwin half-reclines toward her in a supplicating manner. His shepherd's staff and hat lie nearby, guarded by one of his dogs. Close by, four sheep graze under the watchful eyes of a rather heavy-bodied sheepdog. The valley stretches away into the mountains in the center of the picture. In the distance to the left of the mountains, between them and the lovers, a few houses perch on a hillside; opposite these, the columns of a Grecian-style building jut into the right side of the picture. Two doves gaze at each other as they fly toward the trees behind the young couple.

This frontispiece contains two signatures in the lower border. On the bottom left, just barely visible, is "H. Gravelot." On the bottom right is "J. Caldwall, Sculp." "H. Gravelot" is probably Hubert Gravelot (1699–1773), Parisian artist and illustrator who was noted for his delicate and minute skill in book illustrating. He influenced contemporary art in England and was sought after there because of his ability at portrait painting. According to the English *Dictionary of National Biography*, "Gravelot's illustrations are notable for their wealth of grace and fancy, and are executed often in the smallest compass with incredible lightness and delicacy. . . . His designs show both the good and bad taste of the age, and he is seen to better advantage as an illustrator of romance or poetry. . . ." "J. Caldwall" is probably James Caldwall, born in London in 1737. He was a good draftsman and

---

[3] Bibliographically the novel may be described as: Vol I, pages xxiv–178, signatures A-H^{12}, I^6. Vol II, 175 pages, signatures [A^2], B-H^{12}, I^4. In Vol I, pp [i]–xxiv, signatures A^1-B^1, consist of half-title, frontispiece, title page, contents, and eight leaves of preface. In Vol II the half-title and the title page are not included in the pagination. The letterpress size is 2^7/$_{16}$ x 4½″. The title page is: IMOGEN: | A | PASTORAL ROMANCE. | IN TWO VOLUMES. | FROM THE | ANCIENT BRITISH. | tapered rule | Vol. I. | tapered rule | LONDON | PRINTED FOR WILLIAM LANE, | LEADENHALL-STREET. | MDCCLXXXIV.

engraved brilliantly in line. He also was known for his portraits of the aristocracy. He engraved the figures in "The Immortality of Garrick," after G. Carter, in 1783. Gravelot died in 1773; so the drawing was obviously not made for *Imogen*. Caldwall's engravings are dated as late as 1789, however; he may or may not have prepared this plate for its present purpose. Lane would have been following a hoary tradition if he "borrowed" the *Imogen* frontispiece from an earlier work.

Godwin wrote prefaces for all of his novels. He had issued *Caleb Williams* without a preface in the first edition, it is true. That novel had been written during the period of witch-hunting and treason trials by government officials apprehensive that the French Revolution might spread to England, and Godwin's preface had been withdrawn because of the "alarms of the booksellers" who "feared that even the humble novelist, might be shown to be constructively a traitor." But it was printed in later editions. In these prefaces Godwin frequently discussed the sources of his plots, seriously and candidly. In the preface to *Imogen*, however, he wrote almost entirely with tongue in cheek. Though Godwin has been accused of lacking a sense of humor, he enjoyed a wry joke at the expense of reviewers and careless readers. He exhibited this penchant in his earlier *Herald of Literature*, finished in late 1783, which contains reviews of works not yet published. He does a somewhat similar thing in the preface to *Imogen* when he says first that the novel was written by Cadwallo in Welsh, which he translated, then that the novel was written by Rice ap Thomas, who lived during the reign of William III. Actually Rice ap Thomas lived from 1449–1526, while William III lived from 1650–1702. Godwin must have enjoyed the fact that none of the reviewers pointed out this discrepancy.

The extended parody of the contemporary Ossianic tradition in the preface and the pose that the manuscript is a translation from the Welsh of a Romance of Druidical times which might have served as a source of Milton's *Comus*, though not seriously maintained by Godwin, must have appealed to the popular interest in the past. These also show that Godwin was temperamentally a romantic, and the novel's importance is enhanced as another work of Pre-romantic times.

By the numerous authors and works he mentions in the preface, Godwin exhibits a wide knowledge of pastoral literature from Greek to modern times. His use of the Druid mythology in the novel shows that in the Eighteenth Century controversy between those who favored sources from the Greek and Latin pastoral models for their romances and those who argued that the sources ought to be in the native mythology, he agreed with the latter.

His major source of inspiration is, of course, Milton. He bases the plot of the novel on Milton's *Comus*, but there are references to other works by the poet in the novel. "The great Milton," as Godwin calls him in the preface, was always one of Godwin's favorite authors, and his library contained numerous editions of Milton's works.

Though the novel is based on *Comus*, it by no means follows Milton's plot exactly. Basic to both works is the attempt by an evil being to seduce a beautiful, innocent maid, but Godwin introduces a very un-Miltonic love theme. Indeed Imogen's love for Edwin is almost as sustaining as her virtue. The setting of the novel is a beautiful valley in Wales, which Godwin describes with an exactness that can be checked in Baedeker, whereas the setting of the *Masque* is a deep wood. In the novel, Roderic, Comus's counterpart, abducts Imogen in broad day by the aid of a magical storm; in *Comus*, the lady and her brothers become separated and lost in the dark woods. Roderic steals Imogen after careful planning and with the aid of Medoro (the name is the same as that of a character in *Orlando Furioso*); in *Comus*, the evil spirit senses her approach in the woods. Comus wants to add her to the rout of monsters in his power; Roderic's interest is sensual, and he wants Imogen as his mistress. Roderic, though he has magical powers, is far more human than Comus. Here Godwin's interest in the mental state of character, which is so central in his later novels, produces a radical alteration in the theme that innocence can withstand evil: Roderic's peevish complaints that he has money and magical power but cannot seduce Imogen reduce him to the human level. Roderic's dissatisfaction with his actual powerlessness strengthens the theme of the triumphs of the innocence, happiness, and purity of the inhabitants of the valley of the Clwyd over the evil of power and magic. Godwin's most notable handling of the theme that possessions cannot buy happiness for an egocentric individual is found in *Caleb Williams*. Falkland cannot be happy with his money and property; like Roderic, he is hampered because he is a sensitive man with a conscience. Falkland is a far more complex and interesting character than the profligate Roderic, but the basic theme is the same.

Roderic's less-than-absolute power is emphasized by the Adversary who, Discord-like, appears at crucial intervals to warn that violent actions on Roderic's part will result in his downfall. Comus has no limitations on his power, though the Attendant Spirit in the *Masque*, like the ancient Druid Madoc of the novel, exercises some control over the magic. Roderic's power and the magnificence of his castle and surrounding romantic gardens with their "air of rudeness and wildness" come from his mother. She is Rodegune, a name Godwin evidently adapts from the *Faerie Queene*. In that poem, Radigund is the Amazonian queen who hates knights, conquers them, and then makes them do women's work. Her city is named Radegone. She is eventually killed by the chaste Britomart (*Faerie Queene*, V, iv–vii). Roderic's attendant Medoro had been his mother's helper. Rodogune's relationship to Medoro was like that of Prospero and Caliban. Like Caliban, Medoro had a voice "that nature had made up of dissonance and horror" (below, p 75). Roderic's human qualities and his dependence on the help of others blunt the effect of the magic in the story and make him more believable as a novelistic character.[4]

A major difference between *Comus* and the novel is in Godwin's use of a classic pastoral setting in Druidical times. He mentions some classical authors of the pastoral in the preface, and some aspects of his novel are obviously derived from these sources. The innocence of Edwin and Imogen is like the early innocence of Daphnis and Chloe; the musical banquet scenes and the association of the peasants as happy shepherds seem to have been taken from classical models. The pursuit of the daughter of Cadwallo by Modred, in the bard's story in the early part of *Imogen*, is a variation of the Apollo-Daphne theme as well as an admirably contrived preview of the main plot of the novel. In the final inset story, Godwin borrows from such sources as the Bible, *Paradise Lost*, and Du Bartas' *Divine Weeks and Works*. One detail in this story by the ancient Druid Llewellyn, however, suggests a passage in Gessner's *The Death of Abel*: Llewellyn, speaking of creation, mentions "A disdainful horse [which] shook its flowing mane, and snuffed the enlivening breeze, and stretched along the plain" (below, p 36). In Gessner (in Mary Collyer's translation, 12th edition, 1780, p 9) "The new form'd horse bounds o'er the verdant turf, and neighing shakes his mane. . . ."

Godwin's use of the druidical past in the novel was undoubtedly stimulated by the revival of interest in druidic lore as part of the Pre-romantic interest in the past. Such works as Gray's "The Bard" are evidence of this. And Godwin could have looked at such books as John Toland's *A Critical History of the Celtic Religion and Learning: Containing an Account of the*

---

[4] The *Faerie Queene* lies behind both the *Masque* and *Imogen*. Godwin may have gone to Spenser for such an incident as the abduction of Imogen early in the novel. This may have been suggested to him by Proteus' putting Florimell in his chariot. After the abduction, he, like Roderic, tries to seduce his victim. Also like Roderic he later uses disguise in his evil attempts (III, viii). Of course, the use of disguise is a commonplace of eighteenth-century novel and drama, and abductions were frequently reported in the daily newspapers. Sir Guyon's visit to the Bower of Bliss (*Faerie Queene*, III, v) is like Edwin's visit to Roderic's castle at the conclusion of *Imogen*. Music and the enticement of beautiful women are common to both. The song praising womankind in the novel (II 6–11) is similar to the one in the *Faerie Queene*, III, v.

Druids (1720); William Cooke's *An Enquiry into the Patriarchal and Druidical Religion, Temples* (1754), John Smith's *Galic Antiquities: Consisting of a History of the Druids* (1780), or Hugh Blair's recent *Dissertation on the Poems of Ossian, the Son of Fingal* (1783), which contains remarks about primitive English societies.

In any event, Godwin's novel is full of druidical mythology. The sacrifice to the gods, the veneration of the bards, and the sacredness of the oak and the teachings of the prophets are all incorporated. Godwin's originality in the novel lies in the association of this lore and contemporary moral didacticism with the *Comus* plot.

Godwin's druidical society is an ideal society which dwells in a valley isolated from modern evils. In this ideal location

> all was rectitude and guileless truth. The hoarse din of war had never reached its happy bosom; its river had never been impurpled with the stain of human blood. Its willows had not wept over the crimes of its inhabitants, nor had the iron hand of tyranny taught care and apprehension to seat themselves upon the brow of its shepherds. They were strangers to riches, and to ambition, for they all lived in a happy equality. He was the richest man among them, that could boast of the greatest store of yellow apples and mellow pears. And their only objects of rivalship were the skill of the pipe and the favour of beauty. (p 25)

These people have no knowledge of the "degeneracy of modern times."

The contemplation of the ideal society was an obsession with the people of the latter half of the Eighteenth Century. Whereas their grandparents in the earlier part of the century had been fairly complacent about their society (though Swift and others made disturbing observations), the people of the latter part looked in vain for the ideal. Johnson's Rasselas could not find it in or out of his secluded valley. Goldsmith could not find it in Lissoy — though it apparently had been there earlier — or the American wilderness. But the literature shows a constant seeking for it: in the lives of the American Indian, in the pastoral romances of Greek and Roman times, in the young American colonies, and in the Ossianic and druidical literature.

Godwin never found it, but his important writings from *Imogen* on are a seeking after it. *Caleb Williams* in 1794 with its subtitle (in Godwin's time the main title) "Things as They Are," containing realistic pictures of the tortures of English prisons, the brutality of the law, and the crassness of the gentry, is certainly a warning and a lesson. In *Political Justice*, Godwin had set forth the principles for establishing the good society. Adopt these, and the ideal would be attained. The three works *Imogen, Political Justice,* and

Caleb Williams are in an important way complementary. The first shows the ideal pastoral society man could have; the second analyzes man and his institutions to give the principles on which the ideal could yet be formed; the third shows what has happened in the modern world because of the deviations from these principles.

Godwin's novel has little similarity to Gothic Romance or the sentimental novel, so popular during the latter part of the century. Though Roderic's castle may have some characteristics of the Gothic castle, Godwin does not use these to excite or alarm. Nor does he write the novel with the sentimental intent of wringing the last tear out of any incident. Imogen has the tendency of the eighteenth-century heroine to faint or languish under trial (probably copied straight from life), but she is more level-headed than the usual heroines of the novel of sentiment. Godwin already exhibits in this early novel his tendency to present ideas. As Professor Sherburn says, speaking of Godwin's later novels, "There is a fundamental substratum of thought that is common to all the novels. . . ." [5] Despite its artificiality and weak characterization, *Imogen* has this "substratum of thought." Many of the ideas in *Imogen* reappear in Godwin's later work. The idea that virtue is purer after it has passed through the trial of adversity probably was taken by Godwin from Milton's *Areopagitica*. It occurs in *Political Justice* (1798 II 7) where Godwin says that "adversity is the school, in which all extraordinary virtue must be found." Caleb Williams undergoes the trial and ends miserably because he has not withstood the trials of adversity.

Belief in brotherly love and in the simple life go hand in hand. These are found both in the novel and in *Political Justice,* in the latter being related to the idea of universal benevolence. In *Imogen* the ancient Druid Llewellyn counsels the shepherds to "love, support, and cherish each other" (p 37). *Political Justice* contains a chapter "Of Self-Love and Benevolence" (1798, I 421–438) in which la Rochefoucault's denial of disinterested benevolence is refuted. Both here and in the novel Godwin adopts Shaftesbury's doctrine, in the *Inquiry Concerning Virtue,* that man is inclined by his very constitution to love his neighbors and detest vice.

Godwin's early novel and later works contain the idea that excessive riches are detrimental. Imogen says she has no use for superfluous riches, and even Roderic envies the simple life of the shepherds and would quit his "sumptuous palace and magic arts, for the careless, airy, and unreflecting joys of rural simplicity." In *Political Justice* a general aim of the good society is the abolition of property and a return to the simple society where "There

[5] "Godwin's Later Novels," *Studies in Romanticism* I (Winter 1962) 82.

will be no rich man to recline in indolence, and fatten upon the labour of
his fellows. . . . There will be no persons devoted to the manufacture of
trinkets and luxuries; and none whose office it should be to keep in motion
the complicated machine of government, tax-gatherers, beadles, excisemen,
tide-waiters, clerks and secretaries" (1798 II 482). St Leon, in Godwin's
novel of 1799, says, as he looks at the humble life around him in Switzerland:

> Oh, poverty! . . . if these are the delights that attend thee, willingly will I
> resign the pomp of palaces and the splendour of rank to whoever shall
> deem them worth his acceptance! Henceforth I desire only to dedicate
> myself to the simplicity of nature and the genuine sentiments of the heart.
> . . . Wealth serves no other purpose than to deprave the soul, and adulter-
> ate the fountains of genuine delight. (I 270–271)

Godwin continually associates vice with property and virtue with "honest"
poverty. Property is the bugaboo of his philosophy.

Another idea, the necessity for equality, appears in *Imogen*. The idea had
already appeared in Godwin's *An Account of a Seminary* (1783) in the
words, "The state of society is incontestibly artificial; the power of one man
over another must be always derived from convention, or from contest; by
nature we are equal" (p 2). In *Imogen* when Roderic's retainers ask Imogen
to remain in the castle because her going would displease their master and
lord she retorts: "The gods have made all their rational creatures equal. If
they have made one strong and another weak, it is for the purpose of mutual
benevolence and assistance, and not for that of despotism and oppression"
(p 59). In *Political Justice* Godwin says: "Undoubtedly, we must not permit ourselves to think slightly, of the mischiefs that accrue from a state
of inequality. If it be necessary that the great mass of mankind should be
condemned to slavery, and, stranger still, to ignorance, that a few may be
enlightened, certainly those moralists are not to be blamed, who doubted
whether perpetual rudeness were not preferable to such a gift" (II 491).

Closely associated with equality are freedom and independence. The only
gift Roderic could give Imogen which she would accept is her freedom
(p 64). In *Political Justice*, Godwin says that independence is "the first
principle of virtuous feeling" (II 52). Emily Melville, who has been impris-
oned by her barbarous cousin Tyrell in *Caleb Williams*, says, "I prefer
liberty to wealth" (1794 I 189). Caleb, remembering his life in prison, says:
"Never did man more strenuously prefer poverty with independence to the
artificial allurements of a life of slavery" (III 9–10). In *Fleetwood* (1805)
the old man Ruffigny, speaking about his enforced work in the textile mill
when he was only nine, says that he believes it is better to starve with inde-

pendence than undergo the misery associated with his virtual imprisonment in the factory (II 281). In his *Fables, Ancient and Modern* (2d ed 1805) written for children under the pseudonym Edward Baldwin, Godwin has the hungry wolf in the fable of the wolf and the mastiff say: "Hunger shall never make me so slavish and base, as to prefer chains and blows with a belly-full, to liberty" (I 145).

Godwin's *Imogen: A Pastoral Romance* is an important addition to the Godwin canon. Though it suffers from Godwin's fundamental weakness, the "failure to fuse well such elements as action, persons, and mental states in a style capable of expressing these elements," [6] it is no worse than the hundreds of novels and romances which poured from the presses during the last half of the Eighteenth Century. The readers did not expect realistic fiction nor the natural tone of speech. The authors aimed "at elegance, a rounded 'literary' language, rising at times to impassioned rhetoric, such as never flowed from the lips of human being. . . ." [7] Stylistically, Godwin's early novel is no different from those of the other early novelists. His contemporaries, if the reviewers' statements are typical, found the novel satisfactory.

Writing about the novel, the reviewer for the *Critical Review,* LVIII (Oct 1784) 312, says: "We do not hesitate to pronounce that it abounds with tender sentiments, pleasing description, and an innocent simplicity of manners." The *Monthly Review,* LXXII (March 1785), is more critical, objecting to some of Godwin's figures of speech and the lack of verisimilitude, but concludes: "These little volumes, however, are of a chaste and virtuous tendency; and those who are fond of this style of composition, will find both amusement and instruction from the perusal of them." The writer for the *English Review,* IV (Aug 1784) 312, is most laudatory. He says, "the work abounds in beauties, in tender incidents, and simply [sic] pathetic descriptions. It leaves a pleasing impression, and is calculated to revive ideas of the days of pastoral purity and innocence. There is also an agreeable variety, romance, and morality, which cannot fail to recommend it to the young reader." Since Godwin was writing for the *English Review* at this time, possibly the reviewer was attempting to please the author or, as often happened, the author wrote the review himself. *Imogen* was advertised for sale in the daily newspapers: once in the *Morning Chronicle and London Advertiser* on Oct 26 1784; and twice in the *Morning Herald and Daily Advertiser* on July 15 and Nov 29 1784.

---

[6] Sherburn, p 78. — But Sherburn gives Godwin credit for superior ability in handling these elements separately.

[7] Tompkins, p 358.

The last contemporary comment on *Imogen* was Mary Shelley's in her fragment of a biography of her father. She says that this novel is "a forced & fictitious pastoral." Then, writing about his three early novels, she says: "These tales developed his style; he acquired energy & force and eloquence — he became capable of expressing in fitting language the thoughts that arose in his mind. The next thing necessary was a subject, worthy of his genius — a subject to support his style, which hitherto had supported his subject; that did not present itself so readily — & several years passed before Caleb Williams was conceived — and those ideas which were yet as it were in chaos, assumed the shape which still haunts the world with forms of power & excellence." [8]

JACK W. MARKEN

Slippery Rock State College

A NOTE ON THE TEXT

The original text of *Imogen: A Pastoral Romance* was printed with a good many errors. The possessive is frequently omitted; words are occasionally misspelled — or oddly spelled (chesnut, p 30; threatner, p 47; Farewel, p 58; sheers, p 65, etc; and perhaps neighing rock, p 43, is a misprint for "neighboring rock"); a word may be omitted ("In order to this," p 46); and some awkward sentences and mental lapses occur (toward the end of the novel Imogen, though seated in a garden, is described as "advancing toward the door" and as leaving the "apartment"). I have pointed out very few of these errors in the text. I have corrected none of them, preferring to reproduce the text exactly as it was printed.

[8] Quoted from the Abinger manuscripts.

Imogen: A Pastoral Romance

From the Ancient British

1784

Preface

[*By* WILLIAM GODWIN]

THE following performance, as the title imports, was originally composed in the Welch language. Its style is elegant and pure. And if the translator has not, as many of his brethren have done, suffered the spirit of the original totally to evaporate, he apprehends it will be found to contain much novelty of conception, much classical taste, and great spirit and beauty in the execution. It appears under the name of Cadwallo, an ancient bard, who probably lived at least one hundred years before the commencement of our common æra. The manners of the primitive times seem to be perfectly understood by the author, and are described with the air of a man who was in the utmost degree familiar with them. It is impossible to discover in any part of it the slightest trace of Christianity. And we believe it will not be disputed, that in a country so pious as that of Wales, it would have been next to impossible for the poet, though ever so much upon his guard, to avoid all allusion to the system of revelation. On the contrary, every thing is Pagan, and in perfect conformity with the theology we are taught to believe prevailed at that time.

These reasons had induced us to admit, for a long time, that it was perfectly genuine, and justly ascribed to the amiable Druid. With respect to the difficulty in regard to the preservation of so long a work for many centuries by the mere force of memory, the translator, together with the rest of the world, had already got over that objection in the case of the celebrated Poems of Ossian. And if he be not blinded by that partiality, which the midwife is apt to conceive for the productions, that she is the instrument of bringing into the world, the Pastoral Romance contains as much originality, as much poetical beauty, and is as happily calculated to make a deep impression upon the memory, as either Fingal, or Temora.

The first thing that led us to doubt its authenticity, was the striking resemblance that appears between the plan of the work, and Milton's celebrated Masque at Ludlow Castle. We do not mean however to hold forth this circumstance as decisive in its condemnation. The pretensions of Cadwallo, or whoever was the author of the performance, are very high to originality. If the date of the Romance be previous to that of Comus, it may be truly said of the author, that he soared above all imitation, and derived his merits from the inexhaustible source of his own invention. But Milton, it is well known, proposed some classical model to himself in all his productions. The Paradise Lost is almost in every page an imitation of Virgil, or Homer. The Lycidas treads closely in the steps of the Daphnis and Gallus of Virgil. The Sampson Agonistes is formed upon the model of Sophocles. Even the little pieces, L'Allegro and Il Penseroso have their source in a song of Fletcher, and two beautiful little ballads that are ascribed to Shakespeare. But the classical model upon which Comus was formed has not yet been discovered. It is infinitely unlike the Pastoral Comedies both of Italy and England. And if we

could allow ourselves in that licence of conjecture, which is become almost insep-
arable from the character of an editor, we should say: That Milton having written
it upon the borders of Wales, might have had easy recourse to the manuscript
whose contents are now first given to the public: And that the singularity of pre-
serving the name of the place where it was first performed in the title of his poem,
was intended for an ingenuous and well-bred acknowledgement of the source
from whence he drew his choicest materials.

But notwithstanding the plausibility of these conjectures, we are now inclined
to give up our original opinion, and to ascribe the performance to a gentleman of
Wales, who lived so late as the reign of king William the third. The name of this
amiable person was Rice ap Thomas. The romance was certainly at one time in
his custody, and was handed down as a valuable legacy to his descendants, among
whom the present translator has the honour to rank himself. Rice ap Thomas,
Esquire, was a man of a most sweet and inoffensive disposition, beloved and respected by all his neighbours and tenants, and "passing rich with "sixty" pounds
a year." In his domestic he was elegant, hospitable, and even sumptuous, for the
time and country in which he lived. He was however naturally of an abstemious
and recluse disposition. He abounded in singularities, which were pardoned to
his harmlessness and his virtues; and his temper was full of sensibility, seriousness,
and melancholy. He devoted the greater part of his time to study; and he boasted
that he had almost a complete collection of the manuscript remains of our Welch
bards. He was often heard to prefer even to Taliessin, Merlin, and Aneurim, the
effusions of the immortal Cadwallo, and indeed this was the only subject upon
which he was ever known to dispute with eagerness and fervour. In the midst of
the controversy, he would frequently produce passages from the Pastoral Romance,
as decisive of the question. And to confess the truth, I know not how to excuse
this piece of jockeyship and ill faith, even in Rice ap Thomas, whom I regard as
the father of my family, and the chief ornament of my beloved country.

Some readers will probably however be inclined to apologise for the conduct
of Mr. Thomas, and to lay an equivalent blame to my charge. They will tell me,
that nothing but the weakest partiality could blind me to the genuine air of antiquity with which the composition is every where impressed, and to ascribe it to
a modern writer. But I am conscious to my honesty and defy their malice. So far
from being sensible of any improper bias in favour of my ancestor, I am content
to strengthen their hands, by acknowledging that the manuscript, which I am not
at all desirous of refusing to their inspection, is richly emblazoned with all the dis-
coloration and rust they can possibly desire. I confess that the wording has the
purity of Taliessin, and the expressiveness of Aneurim, and is such as I know of
no modern Welchman who could write. And yet, in spite as they will probably
tell me of evidence and common sense, I still aver my persuasion, that it is the
production of Rice ap Thomas.

But enough, and perhaps too much, for the question of its antiquity. It would
be unfair to send it into the world without saying something of the nature of its
composition. It is unlike the Arcadia of sir Philip Sidney, and unlike, what I have

just taken the trouble of running over, the Daphnis of Gessner. It neither on the one hand leaves behind it the laws of criticism, and mixes together the different stages of civilization; nor on the other will it perhaps be found frigid, uninteresting, and insipid. The prevailing opinion of Pastoral seems to have been, that it is a species of composition admirably fitted for the size of an eclogue, but that either its nature will not be preserved, or its simplicity will become surfeiting in a longer performance. And accordingly, the Pastoral Dramas of Tasso, Guarini, and Fletcher, however they may have been commended by the critics, and admired by that credulous train who clap and stare whenever they are bid, have when the recommendation of novelty has subsided been little attended to and little read. But the great Milton has proved that this objection is not insuperable. His Comus is a master-piece of poetical composition. It is at least equal in its kind even to the Paradise Lost. It is interesting, descriptive and pathetic. Its fame is continually increasing, and it will be admired wherever the name of Britain is repeated, and the language of Britain is understood.

If our hypothesis respecting the date of the present performance is admitted, it must be acknowleged that the ingenious Mr. Thomas has taken the Masque of Milton for a model; and the reader with whom Comus is a favourite, will certainly trace some literal imitations. With respect to any objections that may be made on this score to the Pastoral Romance, we will beg the reader to bear in mind, that the volumes before him are not an original, but a translation. Recollecting this, we may, beside the authority of Milton himself, and others as great poets as ever existed who have imitated Homer and one another at least as much as our author has done Comus, suggest two very weighty apologies. In the first place, imitation in a certain degree, has ever been considered as lawful when made from a different language: And in the second, these imitations come to the reader exaggerated, by being presented to him in English, and by a person who confesses, that he has long been conversant with our greatest poets. The translator has always admired Comus as much as the Pastoral Romance; he has read them together, and been used to consider them as illustrating each other. Any verbal coincidencies into which he may have fallen, are therefore to be ascribed where they are due, to him, and not to the author. And upon the whole, let the imperfections of the Pastoral Romance be what they will, he trusts he shall be regarded as making a valuable present to the connoisseurs and the men of taste, and an agreeable addition to the innocent amusements of the less laborious classes of the polite world.

BOOK the FIRST

CHARACTER OF THE SHEPHERDESS AND HER LOVER.
—FEAST OF RUTHYN.—SONGS OF THE BARDS.

LISTEN, O man! to the voice of wisdom. The world thou inhabitest was not intended for a theatre of fruition, nor destined for a scene of repose. False and treacherous is that happiness, which has been preceded by no trial, and is connected with no desert. It is like the gilded poison that undermines the human frame. It is like the hoarse murmur of the winds that announces the brewing tempest. Virtue, for such is the decree of the Most High, is evermore obliged to pass through the ordeal of temptation, and the thorny paths of adversity. If, in this day of her trial, no foul blot obscure her lustre, no irresolution and instability tarnish the clearness of her spirit, then may she rejoice in the view of her approaching reward, and receive with an open heart the crown that shall be bestowed upon her.

The extensive valley of Clwyd once boasted a considerable number of inhabitants, distinguished for primeval innocence and pastoral simplicity. Nature seemed to have prepared it for their reception with all that luxuriant bounty, which characterises her most favoured spots. The inclosure by which it was bounded, of ragged rocks and snow-topt mountains, served but for a foil to the richness and fertility of this happy plain. It was seated in the bosom of North Wales, the whole face of which, with this one exception, was rugged and hilly. As far as the eye could reach, you might see promontory rise above promontory. The crags of Penmaenmawr were visible to the northwest, and the unequalled steep of Snowden terminated the prospect to the south. In its farthest extent the valley reached almost to the sea, and it was intersected, from one end to the other, by the beautiful and translucent waters of the river from which it receives its name.

In this valley all was rectitude and guileless truth. The hoarse din of war had never reached its happy bosom; its river had never been impurpled with the stain of human blood. Its willows had not wept over the crimes of its inhabitants, nor had the iron hand of tyranny taught care and apprehension to seat themselves upon the brow of its shepherds. They were strangers to riches, and to ambition, for they all lived in a happy equality. He was the richest man among them, that could boast of the greatest store of yellow apples and mellow pears. And their only objects of rivalship were the skill of the pipe and the favour of beauty. From morn to eve they tended their fleecy possessions. Their reward was the blazing hearth, the nut-brown beer, and the merry tale. But as they sought only the enjoyment of a humble station, and the pleasures of society, their labours were often relaxed. Often did the setting sun see the young men and the maidens of contiguous villages, assembled round the venerable oak, or the wide-spreading beech. The bells rung in the upland hamlets; the rebecs sounded with rude harmony; they danced with twinkling feet upon the level green or listened to the voice of the song, which was now gay and exhilarating, and now soothed them into pleasing melancholy.

Of all the sons of the plain, the bravest, and the most comely, was Edwin. His forehead was open and ingenuous, his hair was auburn, and flowed about his shoulders in wavy ringlets. His person was not less athletic than it was beautiful. With a firm hand he grasped the boar-spear, and in pursuit he outstripped the flying fawn. His voice was strong and melodious, and whether upon the pipe or in the song, there was no shepherd daring enough to enter the lists with Edwin. But though he excelled all his competitors, in strength of body, and the accomplishments of skill, yet was not his mind rough and boisterous. Success had not taught him a despotic and untractable temper, applause had not made him insolent and vain. He was gentle as the dove. He listened with eager docility to the voice of hoary wisdom. He had always a tear ready to drop over the simple narrative of pastoral distress. Victor as he continually was in wrestling, in the race, and in the song, the shout of triumph never escaped his lips, the exultation of insult he was never heard to utter. On the contrary, with mild and unfictitious friendship, he soothed the breast of disappointment, and cheered the spirits of his adversary with honest praise.

But Edwin was not more distinguished among his brother shepherds, than was Imogen among the fair. Her skin was clear and pellucid. The fall of her shoulders was graceful beyond expression. Her eye-brows were arched, and from her eyes shot forth the grateful rays of the rising sun. Her waist was slender; and as she ran, she outstripped the winds, and her footsteps were printless on the tender herb. Her mind, though soft, was firm; and though yielding as wax to the precepts of wisdom, and the persuasion of innocence, it was resolute and inflexible to the blandishments of folly, and the sternness of despotism. Her ruling passion was the love of virtue. Chastity was the first feature in her character. It gave substance to her accents, and dignity to her gestures. Conscious innocence ennobled all her reflexions, and gave to her sentiments and manner of thinking, I know not what of celestial and divine.

Edwin and Imogen had been united in the sports of earliest infancy. They had been mutual witnesses to the opening blossoms of understanding and benevolence in each others breasts. While yet a boy, Edwin had often rescued his mistress from the rude vivacity of his playmates, and had bestowed upon her many of those little distinctions which were calculated to excite the flame of envy among the infant daughters of the plain. For her he gathered the vermeil-tinctured pearmain, and the walnut with an unsavoury rind; for her he hoarded the brown filberd, and the much prized earth-nut. When she was near, the quoit flew from his arm with a stronger whirl, and his steps approached more swiftly to the destined goal. With her he delighted to retire from the heat of the sun to the centre of the glade, and to sooth her ear with the gaiety of innocence, long before he taught her to hearken to the language of love. For her sake he listened with greater eagerness to the mirthful relation, to the moral fiction, and to the song of the bards. His store of little narratives was in a manner inexhaustible. With them he beguiled the hour of retirement, and with them he hastened the sun to sink behind the western hill.

But as he grew to manly stature, and the down of years had begun to clothe his blushing cheek, he felt a new sensation in his breast hitherto unexperienced. He could not now behold his favourite companion without emotion; his eye sparkled when he approached her; he watched her gestures; he hung upon her accents; he was interested in all her motions. Sometimes he would catch the eye of prudent age or of sharp-sighted rivalry observing him, and he instantly became embarrassed and confused, and blushed he knew not why. He repaired to the neighbouring wake, in order to exchange his young lambs and his hoard of cheeses. Imogen was not there, and in the midst of traffic, and in the midst of frolic merriment he was conscious to a vacancy and a listlessness for which he could not account. When he tended his flocks, and played upon his slender pipe, he would sink in reverie, and form to himself a thousand schemes of imaginary happiness. Erewhile they had been vague and general. His spirit was too gentle for him not to represent to himself a fancied associate; his heart was not narrow enough to know so much as the meaning of a solitary happiness. But Imogen now formed the principal figure in these waking dreams. It was Imogen with whom he wandered beside the brawling rill. It was Imogen with whom he sat beneath the straw-built shed, and listened to the pealing rain, and the hollow roaring of the northern blast. If a moment of forlornness and despair fell to his lot, he wandered upon the heath without his Imogen, and he climbed the upright precipice without her harmonious voice to cheer and to animate him. In a word, passion had taken up her abode in his guileless heart before he was aware of her approach. Imogen was fair; and the eye of Edwin was enchanted. Imogen was gentle; and Edwin loved.

Simple as was the character of the inhabitants of this happy valley, it is not to be supposed that Edwin found many obstacles to the enjoyment of the society of his mistress. Though strait as the pine, and beautiful as the gold-skirted clouds of a summer morning, the parents of Imogen had not learned to make a traffic of the future happiness of their care. They sought not to decide who should be the fortunate shepherd that should carry her from the sons of the plain. They left the choice to her penetrating wit, and her tried discretion. They erected no rampart to defend her chastity; they planted no spies to watch over her reputation. They entrusted her honour to her own keeping. They were convinced, that the spotless dictates of conscious innocence, and that divinity that dwells in virtue and awes the shaggy satyr into mute admiration, were her sufficient defence. They left to her the direction of her conduct. The shepherdess, unsuspicious by nature, and untaught to view mankind with a wary and a jealous eye, was a stranger to severity and caprice. She was all gentleness and humanity. The sweetness of her temper led her to regard with an eye of candour, and her benevolence to gratify all the innocent wishes, of those about her. The character of a woman undistinguishing in her favours, and whose darling employment is to increase the number of her admirers, is in the highest degree unnatural. Such was not the character of Imogen. She was artless and sincere. Her tongue evermore expressed the sentiments of her heart. She drew the attention of no swain from a rival; she employed no stratagems to inveigle the affections; she mocked not the respect of the simple shepherd with delusive encouragement. No man charged her with broken vows; no man could justly accuse her of being cruel and unkind.

It may therefore readily be supposed, that the subject of love rather glided into the conversation of Edwin and Imogen, than was regularly and designedly introduced. They were unknowing in the art of disguising their feelings. When the tale spoke of peril and bravery, the eyes of Edwin sparkled with congenial sentiments, and he was evermore ready to start from the grassy hilloc upon which they sat. When the little narrative told of the lovers pangs, and the tragic catastrophe of two gentle hearts whom nature seemed to have formed for mildness and tranquility, Imogen was melted into the softest distress. The breast of her Edwin would heave with a sympathetic sigh, and he would even sometimes venture, from mingled pity and approbation, to kiss away the tear that impearled her cheek. Intrepid and adventurous with the hero, he began also to take a new interest in the misfortunes of love. He could not describe the passionate complaints, the ingenuous tenderness of another, without insensibly making the case his own. "Had the lover known my Imogen, he would no longer have sighed for one, who could not have been so fair, so gentle, and so lovely." Such were the thoughts of Edwin; and till now Edwin had always expressed his thoughts. But now the words fell half-formed from his trembling lips, and the sounds died away before they were uttered. "Were I to speak, Imogen, who has always beheld me with an aspect of benignity, might be offended. I should say no more than the truth; but Imogen is modest. She does not suspect that she possesses half the superiority over such as are called fair, which I see in her. And who could bear to incur the resentment of Imogen? Who would irritate a temper so amiable and mild? I should say no more than the truth; but Imogen would think it flattery. Let Edwin be charged with all other follies, but let that vice never find a harbour in his bosom; let the imputation of that detested crime never blot his untarnished name."

Edwin had received from nature the gift of an honest and artless eloquence. His words were like the snow that falls beneath the beams of the sun; *they melted as they fell.* Had it been his business to have pleaded the cause of injured innocence or unmerited distress, his generous sympathy and his manly persuasion must have won all hearts. Had he solicited the pursuit of rectitude and happiness, his ingenuous importunity could not have failed of success. But where the mind is too deeply interested, there it is that the faculties are most treacherous. Ardent were the sighs of Edwin, but his voice refused its assistance, and his tongue faultered under the attempts that he made. Fluent and voluble upon all other subjects, upon this he hesitated. For the first time he was dissatisfied with the expressions that nature dictated. For the first time he dreaded to utter the honest wishes of his heart, apprehensive that he might do violence to the native delicacy of Imogen.

But he needed not have feared. Imogen was not blind to those perfections which every mouth conspired to praise. Her heart was not cold and unimpassioned; she could not see these perfections, united with youth and personal beauty, without being attracted. The accents of Edwin were music to her ear. The tale that Edwin told, interested her twice as much as what she heard from vulgar lips. To wander with Edwin along the flowery mead, to sit with Edwin in the cool alcove, had charms for her for which she knew not how to account, and which she was at first unwilling to acknowledge to her own heart. When she heard of the feats of the generous lover, his gallantry in the rural sports, and his reverence for the fair, it was under the amiable figure of Edwin that he came painted to her treacherous imagination. She was a stranger to artifice and disguise, and the renown of Edwin was to her the feast of the soul, and with visible satisfaction she dwelt upon his praise. Even in sleep her dreams were of the deserving shepherd. The delusive pleasures that follow in the train of dark-browed night, all told of Edwin. The unreal mockery of that capricious being, who cheats us with scenes of fictitious wretchedness, was full of the unmerited calamities, the heartbreaking woe, or the untimely death of Edwin. From Edwin therefore the language of love would have created no disgust. Imogen was not heedless and indiscreet; she would not have sacrificed the dignity of innocence. Imogen was not coy; she would not have treated her admirer with affected disdain. She had no guard but virgin modesty and that conscious worth, *that would be wooed, and not unsought be won.*

Such was the yet immature attachment of our two lovers, when an anniversary of religious mirth summoned them, together with their neighbour shepherds of the adjacent hamlet, to the spot which had long been consecrated to rural sports and guiltless festivity, near the village of Ruthyn. The sun shone with unusual splendour; the Druidical temples, composed of immense and shapeless stones, heaped upon each other by a power stupendous and incomprehensible, reflected back his radiant beams. The glade, the place of destination to the frolic shepherds, was shrouded beneath two venerable groves that encircled it on either side. The eye could not pierce beyond them, and the imagination was in a manner embosomed in the vale. There were the quivering alder, the upright fir, and the venerable oak crowned with sacred mistletoe. They grew upon a natural declivity that descended every way towards the plain. The deep green of the larger trees was fringed towards the bottom with the pleasing paleness of the willow. From one of the groves a little rivulet glided across the plain, and was intersected on one side by a stream that flowed into it from a point equally distant from either extremity of its course. Both these streams were bordered with willows. In a word, upon the face of this beautiful spot all appeared tranquility and peace. It was without a path, and you would imagine that no human footsteps had ever invaded the calmness of its solitude. It was the eternal retreat of the venerable anchorite; it was the uninhabited paradise in the midst of the trackless ocean.

Such was the spot where the shepherds and shepherdesses of a hundred cots were now assembled. In the larger compartments of the vale, the more muscular and vigorous swains pursued the flying ball, or contended in the swift-footed race. The bards, venerable for their age and the snowy whiteness of their hair, sat upon a little eminence as umpires of the sports. In the smaller compartments, the swains, mingled with the fair, danced along the level green, or flew, with a velocity that beguiled the eager sight, beneath the extended arms of their fellows. Here a few shepherds, apart from the rest, flung the ponderous quoit that sung along the air. There two youths, stronger and more athletic than the throng, grasped each others arms with an eager hand, and struggled for the victory. Now with manly vigour the one shook the sinewy frame of the other; now they bended together almost to the earth, and now with double force they reared again their gigantic stature. At one time they held each other at the greatest possible distance; and again, their arms, their legs and their whole bodies entwined, they seemed as if they had grown together. When the weaker or less skilful was overthrown, he tumbled like a vast and mountain oak, that for ages had resisted the tumult of the winds; and the whole plain resounded at his fall. Such as were unengaged formed a circle round the wrestlers, and by their shouts and applause animated by turns the flagging courage of either.

And now the sun had gained his meridian height, and, fatigued with labour and heat, they seated themselves upon the grass to partake of their plain and rural feast. The parched wheat was set out in baskets, and the new cheeses were heaped together. The blushing apple, the golden pear, the shining plum, and the rough-coated chesnut were scattered in attractive confusion. Here were the polished cherry and the downy peach; and here the eager gooseberry, and the rich and plenteous clusters of the purple grape. The neighbouring fountain afforded them a cool and sparkling beverage, and the lowing herds supplied the copious bowl with white and foaming draughts of milk. The meaner bards accompanied the artless luxury of the feast with the symphony of their harps.

The repast being finished, the company now engaged in those less active sports, that exercise the subtility of the wit, more than the agility or strength of the body. Their untutored minds delighted themselves in the sly enigma, and the quaint conundrum. Much was their laughter at the wild guesses of the thoughtless and the giddy; and great the triumph of the swain who penetrated the mystery, and successfully removed the abstruseness of the problem. Many were the feats of skill exhibited by the dextrous shepherd, and infinite were the wonder and admiration of the gazing spectators. The whole scene indeed was calculated to display the triumph of stratagem and invention. A thousand deceits were practised upon the simple and unsuspecting, and while he looked round to discover the object of the general mirth, it was increased into bursts of merriment, and convulsive gaiety. At length they rose from the verdant green, and chased each other in mock pursuit. Many flew towards the adjoining grove; the pursued concealed himself behind the dark and impervious thicket, or the broad trunk of the oak, while the pursuers ran this way and that, and cast their wary eyes on every side. Carefully they explored the bushes, and surveyed each clump of tufted trees. And now the neighbouring echoes repeated the universal shout, and proclaimed to the plain below, that the object of their search was found. Fatigue however, in spite of the gaiety of spirit with which their sports were pursued, began to assert his empire, and they longed for that tranquility and repose which were destined to succeed.

At this instant the united sound of the lofty harp, the melodious rebec, and the chearful pipe, summoned them once again to the plain. From every side they hastened to the lawn, and surrounded, with ardent eyes, and panting expectation, the honoured troop of the bards, crowned with laurel and sacred mistletoe. And now they seated themselves upon the tender herb; and now all was stilness and solemn silence. Not one whisper floated on the breeze; not a murmur was heard. The tumultuous winds were hushed, and all was placid composure, save where the gentle zephyr fanned the leaves. The tinkling rill babbled at their feet; the feathered choristers warbled in the grove; and the deep lowings of the distant herds died away upon the ear. The solemn prelude began from a full concert of the various instruments. It awakened attention in the thoughtless, and composed the frolic and the gay into unbroken heedfulness. The air was oppressed with symphonious sounds, and the ear filled with a tumult of harmony.

On a sudden the chorus ceased: Those instruments which had united their force to fill the echoes of every grove, and of every hill, were silent. And now a bard, of youthful appearance, but who was treated with every mark of honour and distinction, and seated on the left hand of the hoary Llewelyn, the prince of song, struck the lyre with a lofty and daring hand. His eye sparkled with poetic rapture, and his countenance beamed with the sublime smile of luxuriant fancy and heaven-born inspiration. He sung of the wanton shepherd, that followed, with ungenerous perseverance, the chaste and virgin daughter of Cadwallo. The Gods took pity upon her distress, the Gods sent down their swift and winged messenger to shield her virtue, and deliver her from the persecution of Modred. With strong and eager steps the ravisher pursued: timid apprehension, and unviolated honour, urged her rapid flight. But Modred was in the pride of youth; muscular and sinewy was the frame of Modred. Beauteous and snowy was the person of the fair: her form was delicate, and her limbs were tender. If heaven had not interposed, if the Gods had not been on her side, she must have fallen a victim to savage fury and brutal lust. But, in the crisis of her fate, she gradually sunk away before the astonished eyes of Modred. That beauteous frame was now no more, and she started from before him, swifter than the winds, a timid and listening hare. Still, still the hunter pursued; he suspended not the velocity of his course. The speed of Modred was like the roe upon the mountains; every moment he gained upon the daughter of Cadwallo. But now the object of his pursuit vanished from his sight, and eluded his eager search. In vain he explored every thicket, and surveyed all the paths of the forest. While he was thus employed, on a sudden there burst from a cave a hungry and savage wolf; it was the daughter of Cadwallo. Modred started with horror, and in his turn fled away swifter than the winds. The fierce and ravenous animal pursued; fire flashed from the eye, and rage and fury sat upon the crest. Mild and gentle was the daughter of Cadwallo; her heart relented; her soft and tender spirit belied the savage form. They approached the far famed stream of Conway. Modred cast behind him a timid and uncertain eye; the virgin passed along, no longer terrible, a fair and milk white hind. Modred inflamed with disappointment, reared his ponderous boar spear, and hurled it from his hand. Too well, ah, cruel and untutored swain! thou levelest thy aim. Her tender side is gored; her spotless and snowy coat is deformed with blood. Agitated with pain, superior to fear, she plunges in the flood. When lo! a wonder; on the opposite

shore she rises, radiant and unhurt, in her native form. Modred contemplates the
prodigy with astonishment; his lust and his brutality inflame him more than ever.
Eagerly he gazes on her charms; in thought he devours her inexpressive beauties.
And now he can no longer restrain himself; with sudden start he leaps into the river.
The waves are wrought into a sudden tempest; they hurry him to and fro. He
buffets them with lusty arms; he rides upon the billows. But vain is human
strength; the unseen messenger of the Gods laughs at the impotent efforts of
Modred. At length the waters gape with a frightful void; the bottom, strewed
with shells, and overgrown with sea-weed, is disclosed to the sight. Modred,
unhappy Modred, sinks to rise no more. His beauty is tarnished like the flower
of the field; his blooming cheek, his crimson lip, is pale and colourless. Learn
hence, ye swains, to fear the Gods, and to reverence the divinity of virtue. Modred
never melted for another's woe; the tear of sympathy had not moistened his cheek.
The heart of Modred was haughty, insolent and untractable; he turned a deaf ear
to the supplication of the helpless, he listened not to the thunder of the Gods.
Let the fate of Modred be remembered for a caution to the precipitate; let the
children of the valley learn wisdom. Heaven never deserts the cause of virtue;
chastity wherever she wanders (*be it not done in pride or in presumption*) is
sacred and invulnerable.

Such was the song of the youthful bard. Every eye was fixed upon his visage
while he struck the lyre; the multitude of the shepherds appeared to have no
faculty but the ear. And now the murmur of applause began; and the wondering
swains seemed to ask each other, whether the God of song were not descended
among them. "Oh glorious youth," cried they, "how early is thy excellence! Ere
manhood has given nerve and vigour to thy limbs, ere yet the flowing beard adorns
thy gallant breast, nature has unlocked to thee her hidden treasures, the Gods
have enriched thee with all the charms of poetry. Great art thou among the bards;
illustrious in wisdom, where they all are wise. Should gracious heaven spare thy
life, we will cease to weep the death of Hoel; we will lament no longer the growing
infirmities of Llewelyn."

While they yet spoke, a bard, who sat upon the right hand of the prince, prepared to sweep the string. He was in the prime of manhood. His shining locks
flowed in rich abundance upon his strong and graceful shoulders. His eye expressed more of flame than gaiety, more of enthusiasm than imagination. His brow,
though manly, and, as it should seem, by nature erect, bore an appearance of
solemn and contemplative. He had ever been distinguished by an attachment to
solitude, and a love for those grand and tremendous objects of uncultivated nature
with which his country abounded. His were the hanging precipice, and the foaming cataract. His ear drank in the voice of the tempest; he was rapt in attention to
the roaring thunder. When the contention of the elements seemed to threaten
the destruction of the universe, when Snowdon bowed to its deepest base, it was
then that his mind was most filled with sublime meditation. His lofty soul soared
above the little war of terrestrial objects, and rode expanded upon the wings of
the winds. Yet was the bard full of gentleness and sensibility; no breast was more
susceptible to the emotions of pity, no tongue was better skilled in the soft and

passionate touches of the melting and pathetic. He possessed a key to unlock all the avenues of the heart.

Such was the bard, and this was the subject of his song. He told of a dreadful famine, that laid waste the shores of the Menai. Heaven, not to punish the shepherds, for, alas, what had these innocent shepherds done? but in the mysterious wisdom of its ways, had denied the refreshing shower, and the soft-descending dew. From the top of Penmaenmaur, as far as the eye could reach, all was uniform and waste. The trees were leafless, not one flower adorned the ground, not one tuft of verdure appeared to relieve the weary eye. The brooks were dried up; their beds only remained to tell the melancholy tale, Here once was water; the tender lambs hastened to the accustomed brink, and lifted up their innocent eyes with anguish and disappointment. The meadows no longer afforded pasture of the cattle; the trees denied their fruits to man. In this hour of calamity the Druids came forth from their secret cells, and assembled upon the heights of Mona. This convention of the servants of the Gods, though intended to relieve the general distress, for a moment increased it. The shepherds anticipated the fatal decree; they knew that at times like this the blood of a human victim was accustomed to be shed upon the altars of heaven. Every swain trembled for himself or his friend; every parent feared to be bereaved of the staff of his age. And now the holy priest had cast the lots in the mysterious urn; and the lot fell upon the generous Arthur. Arthur was beloved by all the shepherds that dwelt upon the margin of the main; the praise of Arthur sat upon the lips of all that knew him. But what served principally to enhance the distress, was the attachment there existed between him and the beauteous Evelina. Mild was the breast of Evelina, unused to encounter the harshness of opposition, or the chilly hand and forbidding countenance of adversity. From twenty shepherds she had chosen the gallant Arthur, to reward his pure and constant love. Long had they been decreed to make each other happy. No parent opposed himself to their virtuous desires; the blessing of heaven awaited them from the hand of the sacred Druid. But in the general calamity of their country they had no heart to rejoice; they could not insult over the misery of all around them. "Soon, oh soon," cried the impatient shepherd, "may the wrath of heaven be overpast! Extend, all-merciful divinity, thy benign influence to the shores of Arvon! Once more may the rustling of the shower refresh our longing ears! Once more may our eyes be gladdened with the pearly, orient dew! May the fields be clothed afresh in cheerful green! May the flowers enamel the verdant mead! May the brooks again brawl along their pebbly bed! And may man and beast rejoice together!" Ah, short-sighted, unapprehensive shepherd! thou dost not know the misfortune that is reserved for thyself; thou dost not know, that thou shalt not live to behold those smiling scenes which thy imagination forestallest; thou dost not see the dart of immature and relentless death that is suspended over thee. Think, O ye swains, what was the universal astonishment and pity, when the awful voice of the Druid proclaimed the decree of heaven! Terror sat upon every other countenance, tears started into every other eye; but the mien of Arthur was placid and serene. He came forward from the throng; his eyes glistened with the fire of patriotism. "Hear me, my countrymen," cried he, "for you

I am willing to die. What is my insignificant life, when weighed against the happiness of Arvon? Be grateful to the Gods, that, for so poor a boon, they are willing to spread wide the hand of bounty, and to exhaust upon your favoured heads the horn of plenty." While he spoke he turned his head to the spot from which he had advanced, and beheld, a melting object, Evelina, pale and breathless, supported in the arms of the maidens. For a moment he forgot his elevated sentiments and his heroism, and flew to raise her. "Evelina, mistress of my heart, awake. Lift up thine eyes and bless thy Arthur. Be not too much subdued by my catastrophe. Live to comfort the grey hairs, and to succour the infirmities of your aged parent." While the breast of Arthur was animated with such sentiments, and dictated a conduct like this, the priests were employed in the mournful preparations. The altar was made ready; the lambent fire ascended from its surface; the air was perfumed with the smoke of the incense; the fillets were brought forth; and the sacred knife glittered in the hand of the chief of the Druids. The bards had strung their harps, and began the song of death. The sounds were lofty and animating, they were fitted to inspire gallantry and enterprise into the trembling coward; they were fitted to breathe a soul into the clay-cold corse. The spirit of Arthur was roused; his eye gleamed with immortal fire. The aged oak, that strikes its root beneath the soil, so defies the blast, and so rears its head in the midst of the whirlwind. But oh, who can paint the distress of Evelina? Now she dropped her head, like the tender lily whose stalk, by some vulgar and careless hand has been broken; and now she was wild and ungovernable, like the wild beast that has been robbed of its young. For an instant the venerable name of religion awed her into mute submission. But when the fatal moment approached, not the Gods, if the Gods had descended in all their radiant brightness, could have restrained her any longer. The air was rent with her piercing cries. She spoke not. Her eyes, in silence turned towards heaven, distilled a plenteous shower. At length, swifter than the winged hawk, she flew towards the spot, and seized the sacred and inviolable arm of the holy Druid, which was lifted up to strike the final blow. "Barbarous and inhuman priest," she cried, "cease your vile and impious mummery! No longer insult us with the name of Gods. If there be Gods, they are merciful; but thou art a savage and unrelenting monster. Or if some victim must expire, strike here, and I will thank thee. Strike, and my bosom shall heave to meet the welcome blow. Do any thing. But oh, spare me the killing, killing spectacle!" During this action the maidens approached and hurried her from the plain. "Go," cried Arthur, "and let not the heart of Evelina be sad. My Death has nothing in it that deserves to be deplored. It is glorious and enviable. It shall be remembered when this frame is crumbled into dust. The song of the bards shall preserve it to never dying fame." The inconsolable fair one had now been forced away. The intrepid shepherd bared his breast to the sacred knife. His nerves trembled not. His bosom panted not. And now behold the lovely youth, worthy to have lived through revolving years, sunk on the ground, and weltering in his blood. Yes, gallant Arthur, thou shalt possess that immortality which was the first wish of thy heart! My song shall embalm thy precious memory, thy generous, spotless fame! But, ah, it is not in the song of the bards to sooth the rooted sorrow of Evelina. Every morning serves only to renew it. Every night she bathes her couch in tears. Those objects, which carry pleasure to the sense of every other fair, serve only to renew thy unexhausted grief. The rustling shower, the pearly dew, the brawling brook, the cheerful green, the flower-enameled mead, all join to tell of the barbarous and untimely fate of Arthur. Smile no more, O ye meads; mock not the grief of Evelina. Let the trees again be leafless; let the rivers flow no longer in their empty beds. A scene like this suits best the settled temper of Evelina.

He ceased. And his pathetic strain had awakened the sympathy of the universal throng. Every shepherd hung his mournful head, when the untimely fate of Arthur was related; every maiden dropped a generous tear over the sorrows of Evelina. They listened to the song, and forgot the poet. Their souls were rapt with alternate passions, and they perceived not the matchless skill by which they were excited. The lofty bard hurried them along with the rapidity of his conceptions, and left them no time for hesitation, and left them no time for reflection. He ceased, and the melodious sounds still hung upon their ear, and they still sat in the posture of eager attention. At length they recollected themselves; and it was no longer the low and increasing murmur of applause: it was the exclamation of rapture; it was the unpremeditated shout of astonishment.

In the mean time, the reverend Llewelyn, upon whose sacred head ninety winters had scattered their snow, grasped the lyre, which had so often confessed the master's hand. Though far advanced in the vale of years, there was a strength and vigour in his age, of which the degeneracy of modern times can have little conception. The fire was not extinguished in his flaming eye; it had only attained that degree of chasteness and solemnity, which had in it by so much the more, all that is majestic, and all that is celestial. His looks held commerce with his native skies. No vulgar passion ever visited his heaven-born mind. No vulgar emotion ever deformed the godlike tranquility of his soul. He had but one passion; it was the love of harmony. He was conscious only to one emotion; it was reverence for the immortal Gods. He sat like the anchorite upon the summit of Snowdon. The tempests raise the foaming ocean into one scene of horror, but he beholds it unmoved. The rains descend, the thunder roars, and the lightnings play beneath his feet.

Llewelyn struck the lyre, and the innumerable croud was noiseless and silent as the chambers of death. They did not now wait for the pleasing tale of a luxuriant imagination, or the pathetic and melting strain of the mourner. They composed their spirits into the serenity of devotion. They called together their innocent thoughts for the worship of heaven. By anticipation their bosoms swelled with gratitude, and their hearts dilated into praise.

The pious Llewelyn began his song from the rude and shapeless chaos. He magnified the almighty word that spoke it into form. He sung of the loose and fenny soil which gradually acquired firmness and density. The immeasurable, eternal caverns of the ocean were scooped. The waters rushed along, and fell with resounding, foamy violence to the depth below. The sun shone forth from his chamber in the east, and the earth wondered at the object, and smiled beneath his beams. Sudden the whole face of it was adorned with a verdant, undulating robe. The purple violet and the yellow crocus bestrewed the ground. The stately oak reared its branchy head, and the trees and shrubs burst from the surface of the earth. Impregnated by power divine, the soil was prolific in other fruits than these. The clods appeared to be informed with a conscious spirit, and gradually assumed a thousand various forms. The animated earth seemed to paw the verdant mead, and to despise the mould from which it came. A disdainful horse, it shook its flowing mane, and snuffed the enlivening breeze, and stretched along the plain. The red-eyed wolf and the unwieldy ox burst like the mole the concealing continent, and threw the earth in hillocs. The stag upreared his branching head. The thinly scattered animals wandered among the unfrequented hills, and cropped the untasted herb. Meantime the birds, with many coloured plumage, skimmed along the unploughed air, and taught the silent woods and hills to echo with their song.

Creatures, hymn the praises of your creator! Thou sun, prolific parent of a thousand various productions, by whose genial heat they are nurtured, and whose radiant beams give chearfulness and beauty to the face of nature, first of all the existences of this material universe acknowledge him thy superior, and while thou dispensest a thousand benefits to the inferior creation, ascribe thine excellencies solely to the great source of beauty and perfection! And when the sun has ceased his wondrous course, do thou, O moon, in milder lustre show to people of a thousand names the honours of thy maker! Thou loud and wintery north wind, in majestic and tremendous tone declare his lofty praise! Ye gentle zephyrs, whisper them to the modest, and softly breathe them in the ears of the lowly! Ye towering pines, and humble shrubs, ye fragrant flowers, and, more than all, ye broad and stately oaks, bind your heads, and wave your branches, and adore! Ye warbling fountains, warbling tune his praise! Praise him, ye beasts, in different strains! And let the birds, that soar on lofty wings, and scale the path of heaven, bear, in their various melody, the notes of adoration to the skies! Mortals, ye favoured sons of the eternal father, be it yours in articulate expressions of gratitude to interpret for the mute creation, and to speak a sublimer and more rational homage.

Heard ye not the music of the spheres? Know ye not the melody of celestial voices? On yonder silver-skirted cloud I see them come. It turns its brilliant lining on the setting day. And these are the accents of their worship. "Ye sons of women, such as ye are now, such once were we. Through many scenes of trial, through heroic constancy, and ever-during patience, have we attained to this bright eminence. Large and mysterious are the paths of heaven, just and immaculate his ways. If ye listen to the siren voice of pleasure, if upon the neck of heedless youth you throw the reins, that base and earth-born clay which now you wear, shall assume despotic empire. And when you quit the present narrow scene, ye shall wear a form congenial to your vices. The fierce and lawless shall assume the figure of the unrelenting wolf. The unreflecting tyrant, that raised a mistaken fame from scenes of devastation and war, shall spurn the ground, a haughty and indignant horse; and in that form, shall learn, by dear experience, what were the sufferings and what the scourge that he inflicted on mankind. The sensual shall wear the shaggy vesture of the goat, or foam and whet his horrid tusks, a wild and untamed boar. But virtue prepares its possessor for the skies. Upon the upright and the good, attendant angels wait. With heavenly spirits they converse. On them the dark machinations of witchcraft, and the sullen spirits of darkness have no power. Even the outward form is impressed with a beam of celestial lustre. By slow, but never ceasing steps, they tread the path of immortality and honour. Then, mortals, love, support, and cherish each other. Fear the Gods, and reverence their holy, white-robed servants. Let the sacred oak be your care. Worship the holy and everlasting mistletoe. And when all the objects that you now behold shall be involved in universal conflagration, and time shall be no more; ye shall mix with Gods, ye shall partake their thrones, and be crowned like them with never-fading laurel."

BOOK the SECOND

THUNDER STORM.—THE RAPE OF IMOGEN.—EDWIN ARRIVES AT THE GROTTO
OF ELWY.—CHARACTER OF THE MAGICIAN.—THE END OF THE FIRST DAY.

THE song of Llewelyn was heard by the shepherds with reverence and mute attention. Their blameless hearts were lifted to the skies with the sentiment of gratitude; their honest bosoms overflowed with the fervour of devotion. They proved their sympathy with the feelings of the bard, not by licentious shouts and wild huzzas, but by the composure of their spirits, the serenity of their countenances, and the deep and unutterable silence which universally prevailed. And now the hoary minstrel rose from the little eminence, beneath the aged oak, from whose branches depended the ivy and the honeysuckle, on which the veneration of the multitude had placed him. He came into the midst of the plain, and the sons and the daughters of the fertile Clwyd pressed around him. Fervently they kissed the hem of his garment; eagerly with their eyes they sought to encounter the benign rays of his countenance. With the dignity of a magistrate, and the tenderness of a father, he lifted his aged arms, and poured upon them his mild benediction. "Children, I have met your fathers, and your fathers fathers, beneath the hills of Ruthyn. Such as they were, such are ye, and such ever may ye remain. The lily is not more spotless, the rose and the violet do not boast a more fragrant odour, than the incense of your prayers when it ascends to the footstool of the Gods. Guileless and undesigning are you as the yeanling lamb; gentle and affectionate as the cooing dove. Qualities like these the Gods behold with approbation; to qualities like these the Gods assign their choicest blessings. My sons, there is a splendour that dazzles, rather than enlightens; there is a heat that burns rather than fructifies. Let not characters like these excite your ambition. Be yours the unfrequented sylvan scene. Be yours the shadowy and unnoticed vale of obscurity. Here are the mild and unruffled affections. Here are virtue, peace and happiness. *Here also are* Gods."

Having thus said, he dismissed the assembly, and the shepherds prepared to return to their respective homes. Edwin and Imogen, as they had come, so they returned together. The parents of the maiden had confided her to the care of the gallant shepherds. "She is our only child," said they, "our only treasure, and our life is wrapt up in her safety. Watch over her like her guardian genius. Bring her again to our arms adorned with the cheerfulness of tranquility and innocence." The breast of Edwin was dilated with the charge; he felt a gentle undulation of pride and conscious importance about his heart, at the honour conferred upon him.

The setting sun now gilded the western hills. His beams played upon their summits, and were reflected in an irregular semi-circle of splendour, spotless and radiant as the robes of the fairies. The heat of the day was over, the atmosphere was mild, and all the objects round them quiet and serene. A gentle zephyr fanned the leaves; and the shadows of the trees, projecting to their utmost length, gave an additional coolness and a soberer tint to the fields through which they passed.

The conversation of these innocent and guileless lovers was, as it were, in unison with the placidness of the evening. The sports, in which they had been engaged, had inspired them with gaiety, and the songs they had heard, had raised their thoughts to a sublimer pitch than was usual to them. They praised the miracles of the tale of Modred; they sympathised with the affliction of Evelina; and they spoke with the most unfeigned reverence of the pious and venerable Llewelyn.

But the harmless chearfulness of their conversation did not last long. The serenity that was around them was soon interrupted, and their attention was diverted to external objects. Suddenly you might have perceived a cloud, small and dark, that rose from the bosom of the sea. By swift advances it became thicker and broader, till the whole heavens were enveloped in its dismal shade. The gentle zephyr, that anon played among the trees, was changed into a wind hollow and tumultuous. Its course was irregular. Now all was still and silent as the caverns of death; and again it burst forth in momentary blasts, or whirled the straws and fallen leaves in circling eddies. The light of day was shrouded and invisible. The slow and sober progress of evening was forestalled. The woods and the hills were embosomed in darkness. Their summits were no longer gilded. One by one the beams of the sun were withdrawn from each; and at length Snowdon itself could not be perceived.

Our shepherd and his charge had at this moment reached the most extensive and unprotected part of the plain. No friendly cot was near to shield them from the coming storm. And now a solemn peal of thunder seemed to roll along over their heads. They had begun to fly, but the tender Imogen was terrified at the unexpected crash, and sunk, almost breathless, into the arms of Edwin. In the mean time, the lightnings seemed to fill the heavens with their shining flame. The claps of thunder grew louder and more frequent. They reverberated from rock to rock, and from hill to hill. If at any time, for a transitory interval, the tremendous echoes died away upon the ear, it was filled with the hollow roaring of the winds, and the boisterous dashing of the distant waves. At length the pealing rain descended. It seemed as if all the waters of heaven were exhausted upon their naked heads. The anxious and afflicted Edwin took his beauteous and insensible companion in his arms, and flew across the plain.

But at this instant, a more extraordinary and terrifying object engrossed his attention. An oak, the monarch of the plain, towards which he bent his rapid course, was suddenly struck with the bolt of heaven, and blasted in his sight. Its large and spreading branches were withered; its leaves shrunk up and faded. In the very trunk a gaping and tremendous rift appeared. At the same moment two huge and craggy cliffs burst from the surrounding rocks, to which they had grown for ages, and tumbling with a hideous noise, trundled along the plain.

At length a third spectacle, more horrible than the rest, presented itself to the affrighted eyes of Edwin. He saw a figure, larger than the human, that walked among the clouds, and piloted the storm. Its appearance was dreadful, and its shape, loose and undistinguishable, seemed to be blended with the encircling darkness. From its coutenance gleamed a barbarous smile, ten times more terrific than the frown of any other being. Triumph, inhuman triumph, glistened in its eye, and, with relentless delight, it brewed the tempest, and hurled the destructive lightning. Edwin gazed upon this astonishing apparition, and knew it for a goblin of darkness. The heart of Edwin, which no human terror could appal, sunk within him; his nerves trembled, and the objects that surrounded him, swam in confusion before his eyes. But it is not for virtue to tremble; it is not for conscious innocence to fear the power of elves and goblins. Edwin presently recollected himself, and a gloomy kind of tranquility assumed the empire of his heart. He was more watchful than ever for his beloved Imogen; he gazed with threefold earnestness upon the fearful spectre.

A sound now invaded his ear, from the shapeless rocks behind him. They repeated it with all their echoes. It was hollow as the raging wind; and yet it was not the raging wind. It was loud as the roaring thunder; and yet it was not the voice of thunder. But he did not remain long in suspense, from whence the voice proceeded. A wolf, whom hunger had made superior to fear, leaped from the rock, upon the plain below. Edwin turned his eyes upon the horrid monster; he grasped his boarspear in his hand. The unconscious Imogen glided from his arms, and he advanced before her. He met the savage in his fury, and plunged his weapon in his side. He overturned the monster; he drew forth his lance reeking with his blood; his enemy lay convulsed in the agonies of death. But ere he could return, he heard the sound of a car rattling along the plain. The reins were of silk, and the chariot shone with burnished gold. Upon the top of it sat a man, tall, lusty, and youthful. His hair flowed about his shoulders, his eyes sparkled with untamed fierceness, and his brow was marked with the haughty insolence of pride. It was Roderic, lord of a hundred hills; but Edwin knew him not. The goblin descended from its eminence, and directed the course of Roderic. In a moment, he seized the breathless and insensible Imogen, and lifted her to his car. Edwin beheld the scene with grief and astonishment; his senses were in a manner overwhelmed with so many successive prodigies. But he did not long remain inactive; grief and astonishment soon gave way to revenge. He took his javelin, still red with the blood of the mountain wolf, and whirled it from his hand. Edwin was skilled to toss the dart; from his hand it flew unerring to its aim. Forceful it sung along the air; but the goblin advanced with hasty steps among the clouds. It touched it with its hand, and it fell harmless and pointless to the ground. During this action the car of Roderic disappeared. The goblin immediately vanished; and Edwin was left in solitude.

The storm however had not yet ceased. The rain descended with all its former fury. The thunder roared with a strong and deafening sound. The lightnings flamed from pole to pole. But the lightnings flamed, and the thunder roared unregarded. The storm beat in vain upon the unsheltered head of Edwin. "Where," cried he, with the voice of anguish and despair, "is my Imogen, my mistress, my wife, the charmer of my soul, the solace of my heart?" Saying this, he sprung away like the roe upon the mountains. His pace was swifter than that of the zephyr when it sweeps along over the unbending corn. He soon reached the avenue by which the chariot had disappeared from his sight. He leaped from rock to rock; he ascended to the summit of the cliff. His eye glanced the swift-flying car of Roderic; he knew him by his gilded carriage, and his spangled vest. But he saw him only for a moment. His aching eye pursued the triumphant flight in vain. "Stay, stay, base ravisher, inglorious coward!" he exclaimed. "If thou art a man, return and meet me. I will encounter thee hand to hand. I will not fear the strength of thy shoulders, and the haughtiness of thy crest. If in such a cause, with the pride of virtue on my side, with all the Gods to combat for me, I am yet vanquished, then be Imogen thine: then let her be submitted to thy despotic power, to thy brutal outrage, and I will not murmur."

But his words were given to the winds of heaven. Roderic fled far, far away. The heart of Edwin was wrung with anguish. "Ye kind and merciful Gods!" exclaimed he, "grant but this one prayer, and the voice of Edwin shall no more importune you with presumptuous vows. Blot from the book of fate the tedious interval. Give me to find the potent villain. Though he be hemmed in with guards behind guards; though his impious mansion strike its foundations deep to the centre, and rear its head above the clouds; though all the powers of hell combine on his side, I will search him out, I will penetrate into his most hidden recess. I can but die. Oh, if I am to be deprived of Imogen, how sweet, how solacing is the thought of death! Let me die in her cause. That were some comfort yet. Let me die in her presence, let her eyes witness the fervour of my attachment, and I will die without a groan."

Having thus poured forth the anguish of his bosom, he resumed the pursuit. But how could Edwin, alone, on foot, and wearied with the journey of the day, hope to overtake the winged steeds of Roderic? And indeed had his speed been tenfold greater than it was, it had been exerted to no purpose. As the ravisher arrived at the edge of the mountain, he struck into a narrow and devious path that led directly to his mansion. But Edwin, who had for some time lost sight of the chariot, took no notice of a way, covered with moss and overgrown with bushes; and pursued the more beaten road. Swift was his course; but the swifter he flew, the farther still he wandered from the object of his search. A rapid brook flowed across his path, which the descending rains had swelled into a river. Without a moment's hesitation, accoutered as he was, he plunged in. Instantly he gained the opposite bank, and divided the air before him, like an arrow in its flight.

In the mean time, the storm had ceased, the darkness was dispersed, and only a few thin and fleecy clouds were scattered over the blue expanse. The sun had for some time sunk beneath the western hills. The heavens, clear and serene, had assumed a deeper tint, and were spangled over with stars. The moon, in calm and silver lustre, lent her friendly light to the weary traveller. Edwin was fatigued and faint. He tried to give vent to his complaints; but his tongue cleaved to the roof of his mouth: his spirits sunk within him. No sound now reached his ears but the baying of the shepherds dogs, and the *drowsy tinklings* of the *distant folds*. The owl, the solemn bird of night, sat buried among the branches of the aged oak, and with her melancholy hootings gave an additional serenity to the scene. At a small distance, on his right hand, he perceived a contiguous object that reflected the rays of the moon, through the willows and the hazels, and chequered the view with a clear and settled lustre. He approached it. It was the lake of Elwy; and near it he discovered that huge pile of stones, so well known to him, which had been reared ages since, by the holy Druids. It was upon this spot that they worshipped the Gods. But they had no habitation near it. They repaired thither at stated intervals from the woods of Mona, and the shores of Arvon. One only Druid lived by the banks of the silver flood, and watched the temple day and night, that no rude hand might do violence to the sanctity of the place, and no profaner mortal, with sacrilegious foot might enter the mysterious edifice. It was surrounded with a wall of oaks. The humbler shrubs filled up their interstices, and there was no avenue to the sacred shade, except by two narrow paths on either side the lake.

The solemn stilness of the scene for a moment hushed the sorrows of Edwin into oblivion. Ah, short oblivion! scarcely had he gazed around him, and drank of the quietness and peace of the scene, ere those recent sorrows impressed his bosom with more anguish than before. Recollecting himself however, he trod the mead with nimble feet, and approached, trembling and with hesitation, to the eastern avenue. "Hear me, sage and generous Madoc," cried the shepherd, with a voice that glided along the peaceful lake, "hear the sorrows of the most forlorn of all the sons of Clwyd!" The hermit, who sat at the door of his grotto, perceived the sound, and approached to the place from which it proceeded. The accent was gentle; and he feared no boisterous intrusion. The accent was tender and pathetic; and never was the breast of Madoc steeled against the voice of anguish. "Approach, my son," he cried. "What disastrous event has brought thee hither, so far from thy peaceful home, and at this still and silent hour of night? Has any lamb wandered from thy fold, and art thou come hither in pursuit of it?" Edwin was silent. His heart seemed full almost to bursting, and he could not utter a word. "Hast thou wandered from thy companions and missed the path that led to the well-known hamlet?" "Alas," said Edwin, "I had a companion once!" and he lifted up his eyes to heaven in speechless despair. "Has thy mistress deserted thee, or have her parents bestowed her on some happier swain?" "Yes," said Edwin, "I have lost her, who was dear to me as the *ruddy drops that visit my sad heart*. But she was constant. Her parents approved of my passion, and consigned her to my arms." "Has sickness then overtaken her, or has untimely death put a period to thy prospects, just as they began to bloom?" "Oh, no," said the disconsolate shepherd, "I have encountered a disaster more comfortless and wasteful than sickness. I had a thousand times rather have received her last sigh, and closed her eyes in darkness!"

During this conversation, they advanced along the banks of Elwy, and drew towards the grotto of the hermit. The hospitable Madoc brought some dried fruits and a few roots from his cell, and spread them before his guest. He took a bowl of seasoned wood, and hastening to the fountain, that fell with a murmuring noise down the neighing [sic] rock, he presented the limpid beverage. "Such," said he, "is my humble fare; partake it with a contented heart, and it shall be more grateful to thy taste, than the high flavoured viands of a monarch." In the mean time, Madoc, pleased with the benevolent pursuit, gathered some bits of dry wood, and setting them on fire, besought the swain to refresh himself from the weariness of his travel, and the inclemency of the storm. But the heart of Edwin was too full to partake of the provisions that his attentive host had prepared. The chearfulness however of the blazing hearth and the generous officiousness of the hermit, seemed by degrees to recover him from the insensibility and lethargy, that for a time had swallowed up all his faculties.

Madoc had hitherto contemplated his guest in silence. He permitted him to refresh his wearied frame and to resume his dissipated spirits uninterrupted; he suppressed the curiosity by which he was actuated, to learn the story of the woes of Edwin. In the midst of his dejection, he perceived the symptoms of a nobility of spirit that interested him; and the anguish of the shepherd's mind had not totally destroyed the traces of that mild affability, and that manly frankness for which he was esteemed.

Edwin had no sooner appeared to shake off a small part of his melancholy, his eye no sooner sparkled with returning fire, than Madoc embraced the favourable omen. "My son," said he, "you seem to be full of dejection and grief. Grief is not an inmate of the plain; the hours of the shepherd are sped in gaiety and mirth. Suspicion and design are stranger to his bosom. With him the voice of discord is not heard. The scourge of war never blasted his smiling fields; the terror of invasion never banished him from the peaceful cot. You too are young and uninured even to the misfortunes of the shepherd. No contagion has destroyed your flock; no wolf has broken its slender barriers: you have felt the anguish of no wound, and been witness to the death of no friend. Say then, my son, why art thou thus dejected and forlorn?"

"Alas," replied Edwin, "our equal lot undoubtedly removes us from the stroke of many misfortunes; but even to us adversity extends its rod. I have been exposed to the ravages of an invader, more fearful than the wolf, more detested than the conqueror. From an affliction like mine, no occupation, no rank, no age can exempt. Sawest thou not the descending storm? Did not the rain beat upon thy cavern, and the thunder roar among the hills?" "It did," cried Madoc, "and I was struck with reverence, and worshipped the God who grasps the thunder in his mighty hand. Wast thou, my son, exposed to its fury?" "I was upon the bleak and wide extended heath. With Imogen, the fairest and most constant of the daughters of Clwyd, I returned from the feast of Ruthyn. But alas," added the shepherd, "the storm had no terrors, when compared with the scenes that accompanied it. I beheld, Madoc, nor are the words I utter the words of shameless imposition, or coward credulity; I beheld a phantom, that glided along the air, and rode among the clouds. At his command, a wolf from the forest, with horrid tusks, and eyes of fire, burst upon me. I advanced towards it, that I might defend the fairest of her sex from its fury, and plunged my javelin in its heart. But, oh! while I was thus engaged, a chariot advanced on the opposite side! Its course was directed by the spectre. The rider descended on the plain, and seized the spotless, helpless Imogen; and never, never shall these eyes behold her more! Such, O thou servant of the Gods, has been my adversity. The powers of darkness have arrayed themselves against me. For me the storm has been brewed; all the arrows of heaven have been directed against my weak, defenceless head. For me the elements have mixed in tremendous confusion; portents and prodigies have been accumulated for my destruction. Oh, then, generous and hospitable Druid, what path is there, that is left for my deliverance? What chance remains for me, now that a host of invisible beings combats against me? Teach me, my friend, my father, what it is that I must do. Tell me, is there any happiness in store for Edwin, or must I sink, unresisting, into the arms of comfortless despair?"

"My son," cried the venerable hermit, "hope is at all times our duty, and despair our crime. It is not in the power of events to undermine the felicity of the virtuous. Goblins, and spirits of darkness, are permitted a certain scope in this terrestrial scene; but their power is bounded; beyond a certain line they cannot wander. In vain do they threaten innocence and truth. Innocence is a wall of brass upon which they can make no impression. Virtue is an adamant that is sacred and secure from all their efforts. He whose thoughts are full of rectitude and heaven, who knows no guile, may wander in safety through uncultivated forests, or sandy plains, that have never known the trace of human feet. Before him the robber is just, and the satyr tame; for him the monsters of the desert are disarmed of their terrors, and he shall lead the wild boar and the wolf in his hand. Such is the sanctity that heaven has bestowed on unblemished truth."

"Alas, my father," cried Edwin, "this is the lesson that was first communicated to my childhood; and my infant heart bounded with the sacred confidence it inspired. But excuse the presumption of a distracted heart. This lesson, to which at another time I could have listened with rapture and enthusiasm, seems now too loose and general for a medicine to my woes. Innocence the Gods have made superior and invulnerable. And, oh, in what have I transgressed? Yet, my father, I am wounded in the tenderest part. Shall I ever recover my Imogen? Is she not torn from me irreversibly? How shall I engage with powers invisible, and supernatural? How shall I discover my unknown, human enemy? No, Madoc, I am lost in impenetrable darkness. For me there is no hope, no shadow of approaching ease."

"Be calm, my son," rejoined the anchorite. "Arrogance and impatience become not the weak and uninformed children of the earth. Be calm, and I will administer a remedy more appropriate to your wrongs. But remember this is your hour of trial. If now you forget the principles of your youth, and the instructions of the sacred Druids, you shall fall from happiness, never to regain it more. But if you come forth pure and unblemished from the fierce assay, your Imogen shall be yours, the Gods shall take you into their resistless protection, and in all future ages, when men would cite an example of distinguished felicity, they shall say, as fortunate as Edwin of the vale." Edwin bended his knee in mute submission.

"Listen, my son," continued the Druid. "I know your enemy, and can point out to you his obscure retreat." The shepherd lifted up his eyes, lately so languid, that now flashed with fire. He eagerly grasped the hand of Madoc. "Alas," continued the hermit, "to know him would little answer the purpose of thy bold and enterprising spirit. They adversary, as thou mayest have conjectured, is in league with the powers of darkness. Against them what can courage, what can adventure avail? They can unthread thy joints, and crumble all thy sinews. They can chain up thy limbs in marble. For how many perils, how many unforseen disasters ought he to be prepared, who dares to encounter them?"

"The name of him who has ravished from thee the dearest treasure of thy heart, is Roderic. His mother — attend, oh Edwin, for whatever the incredulous may pretend, the tales related by the bards in their immortal songs, of ghosts, and fairies, and dire enchantment, are not vain and fabulous. — You have heard of the inauspicious fame and the bad eminence of Rodogune. She withdrew from the fields of Clwyd within the memory of the elder of shepherds. Various were the conjectures occasioned by her disappearance. Some imagined, that for the haughtiness of her humour, and the malignity of her disposition, characters that were wholly unexampled in the pastoral life, she had been carried away before the period limited by nature to the place of torment by the goblins of the abyss. Others believed that she concealed herself in the top of the highest mountain that was near them, and by a commerce with invisible, malignant beings, still exercised the same gloomy temper in more potent, and therefore more inauspicious harm. The blight that overspread the meadows, the destructive contagion that diffused itself among the flocks, the raging tempest that rooted up the oak, when the thunder roared among the hills, and the lightning flashed from pole to pole, they ascribed to the machinations and the sorcery of Rodogune. Their conjectures indeed were blind, but their notions were not wholly mistaken.

"Rodogune was the mother of Roderic. She was deeply skilled in those dark and flagitious arts, which have cast a gloom upon this mortal scene. The intellectual powers bestowed upon her by the Gods were great and eminent, and were given for a far different purpose than to be employed in these sinister pursuits. But all conspicuous talents are liable, my son, to base perversion; and such was the fate of those of Rodogune. She delighted in the actions which her dark and criminal alliance with invisible powers enabled her to perform. It was her's to mislead the benighted shepherd. It was her's to part the happy lovers. For this purpose she would swell the waves, and toss the feeble bark. She dispensed, according to the dictates of her caprice, the mildew among the tender herb, and the pestilence among the folds of the shepherds. By the stupendous powers of enchantment, she raised from the bosom of a hill a wondrous edifice. The apartments were magnificent and stately; unlike the shepherd's cot, and not to be conceived by the imagination of the rustic. Here she accumulated a thousand various gratifications; here she wantoned in all the secret and licentious desires of her heart. But her castle was not merely a scene of thoughtless pleasure. Within its circle she held crouds of degenerate shepherds, groveling through the omnipotence of her incantations in every brutal form. Even the spectres and the elves that disobeyed her authority, she held in the severest durance. She compressed their tender forms in the narrowest prison, or gave them to the stormy winds, to be whirled, *with restless violence, round about* the ample globe. In a word, her mansion was one uninterrupted scene of ingenious cruelty and miserable despair. To be surrounded with the face of disappointment and agony was the happiness of Rodogune.

"When first by her art she raised that edifice which is now inhabited by her son, she had been desirous to conceal it from the prying eyes of the wanderer. In order to this, though it stood upon an eminence, she chose an eminence that was surrounded by higher hills, and hills which, according to the neighbouring shepherds, were impassable. No adventurous step had ever since the day they were created pierced beyond them. It was imagined that the space they surround-ed was the haunt of elves, and the resort of those who held commerce with evil spirits. The curling smoke, which of late has frequently been seen to ascend from their bosom, has confirmed this tradition. And in order to render her habitation still more impervious, Rodogune surrounded it with a deep grove of oaks, whose thick branches entwined together, permitted no passage so much as to the light of day.

"Roderic was her only child, the darling of her age, and the central object of all her cares. At his birth the elves and the fairies were summoned together. They bestowed upon him every beauty of person and every subtlety of wit. To every weapon they made him invulnerable. And, without demanding from him that care and persevering study, that had planted wrinkles on his mother's brow, they gave him to enjoy his wishes instantly and uncontroled. One only goblin was daring enough to pronounce a curse upon him. "When Roderic," cried he, "Shall be Overreached in all His Spells by a Simple Swain, Unversed in the Various Arts of Sorcery and Magic: When Roderic Shall Sue to a Simple Maid, Who by His Charms Shall be Made to Hate the Swain That Once She Loved, and Who Yet Shall Resist all His Personal Attractions and all His Power; Then Shall His Power be at an End. His Palaces Shall be Dissolved, His Riches Scattered, and He Himself Shall Become an Unpitied, Necessitous, Miserable Vagabond." Such was the mysterious threat; and dearly did the threatner abide it. In the mean time, an elf more generous, more attached to Rodogune, and more potent than the rest, bestowed upon the infant a mysterious ring. By means of this he is empowered to assume what form he pleases. By means of this it was hoped he would be able to subdue the most prepossessed, and melt the most obdurate female heart. By means of this it was hoped, he might evade not only the simple swain, but all the wiles of the most experienced and subtle adversary.

"Roderic now increased in age, and began to exhibit the promises of that manly and graceful beauty that was destined for him. He inherited his mother's haughti-ness, and his wishes and his passions were never subjected to contradiction. A few years since that mother died, and the youth has been too much engaged in volup-tuousness and luxury to embark in the malicious pursuits of Rodogune. Sensuality has been his aim, and pleasure has been his God. To gratify his passions has been the sole object of his attentions; and he has remitted no exertion that could enhance to him the joys of the feast and the fruition of beauty. One low-minded gratification has succeeded to another; pleasures of an elevated and intellectual kind have been strangers to his heart; and were it not that the subtlety of wit was a gift bestowed upon him by supernatural existencies, he must long ere this have sunk his mind to the lowest savageness and the most contemptible imbecility."

Edwin heard the tale of the Druid with the deepest attention. He was interested in the information it contained; he was astonished at the unfathomable witcheries of Rodogune; and he could not avoid the being apprehensive of the unexpanded powers of Roderic. But the daring and adventurous spirit of youth, and the anxiety that he felt for the critical situation of Imogen, soon overpowered and obliterated

these impressions. The Druid finished; and he started from his seat. "Point me,
kind and generous Madoc, to the harbour of the usurper. I will invade his palace.
I will enter fearlessly the lime-twigs of his spells. I will trust in the omnipotency of
innocence. Though the magician should be encircled with all the horrid forms
that ingenious fear ever created, though all the grizly legions of the infernal realm
should hem in, I will find him out, and force him to relinquish his prize, or drag
him by his shining hair to a death, ignominious and accursed, as has been the
conduct of his life."

The Druid assumed a sterner and a severer aspect. "How long, son of the valley,"
cried he, "wilt thou be deaf to the voice of instruction? When wilt thou temper
thy heedless and inconsiderate courage with the coolness of wisdom and the
moderation of docility? But go," added he, "I am to blame to endeavour to
govern thy headlong spirit, or stem the torrent of youthful folly. Go, and endure
the punishment of thy rashness. Encounter the magician in the midst of his spells.
Expose thy naked and unprotected head to glut his vengeance. Over thy life
indeed, he has no power. Deliberate guilt, not unreflecting folly, can deprive thee
of thy right to that. But, oh, shepherd, what avails it to live in hopeless misery?
With ease he shall shut thee up for revolving years in darkness tangible; he shall
plunge thee deep beneath the surface of the mantled pool, the viscous spume
shall draw over thy miserable head its dank and dismal shroud; or perhaps, more
ingenious in mischief, he shall chain thee up in inactivity, a conscious statue, the
silent and passive witness of the usurped joys that once thou fondly fanciedst thy
own."

"Oh, pardon me, sage and venerable Madoc," replied the shepherd. "Edwin
did not come from the hands of nature obstinate and untractable. But grief agi-
tates my spirits; anxiety and apprehension conjure up a thousand horrid phantoms
before my distracted imagination, and I am no longer myself. I will however
subdue my impatient resentments. I will listen with coolness to the voice of native
sagacity and hoary experience. Tell me then, my father, and I will hearken with
mute attention, nor think the lesson long, — instruct me how I shall escape those
tremendous dangers thou hast described. Say, is there any remedy, canst thou
communicate any potent and unconquerable amulet, that shall shield me from
the arts of sorcery? Teach me, and my honest heart shall thank thee. Communicate
it, and the benefit shall be consecrated in my memory to everlasting gratitude."

"My son," replied Madoc, "I am indeed interested for thee. Thy heart is ingenuous and sincere; thy misfortune is poignant and affecting. Listen then to my
directions. Receive and treasure up this small and sordid root. In its external
appearance, it is worthless and despicable; but, Edwin, we must not judge by
appearances; that which is most valuable often delights to shroud itself under a
coarse and unattractive outside. In a richer climate, and under a more genial sun,
it bears a beauteous flower, whose broad leaves expand themselves to the day,
and are clothed with a deep and splendid purple, glossy as velvet, and bedropped
with gold. This root is a sovereign antidote against all blasts, enchantments, witch-
crafts, and magic. With this about thee, thou mayest safely enter the haunts of
Roderic; thou mayest hear his incantations unappalled; thou mayest boldly dash

from his hand his magic glass, and shed the envenomed beverage on the ground. Then, when he stands astonished at the unexpected phenomenon, wrest from him his potent wand. Invoke not the unhallowed spirits of the abyss; invoke the spotless synod of the Gods. Strike with his rod the walls of his palace, and they shall turn to viewless air; the monster shall be deprived of all his riches, and all his accumulated pleasures; and thou and thy Imogen, delivered from the powers of enchantment, shall be, for one long, uninterrupted day, happy in the enjoyment of each other.

"Attend, my son, yet attend, to one more advice, upon which all thy advantage and all thy success in this moment of crisis hang. Engage not in so arduous and important an enterprise immaturely. Thou hast yet no reason for despair. Thou art yet beheld with favour by propitious heaven. But thou mayest have reason for despair. One false step may ruin thee. One moment of heedless inconsideration may plunge thee in years of calamity. One moment of complying guilt may shut upon thee the door of enjoyment and happiness for ever."

Such was the sorrow, and such were the consolations of Edwin. But far different was the situation, and far other scenes were prepared for his faithful shepherdess. For some time after she had been seized by Roderic, she had remained unconscious and supine. The terrors that had preceded the fatal capture, had overpowered her delicate frame, and sunk her into an alarming and obstinate fit of insensibility. They had now almost reached the palace of the magician, when she discovered the first symptoms of returning life. The colour gradually remounted into her bloodless cheeks; her hands were raised with a feeble and involuntary motion, and at length she lifted up her head, and opened her languid, unobserving eyes. "Edwin," she cried, "my friend, my companion, where art thou? Where have we been? Oh, it is a long and tedious evening!" Saying this, she looked upon the objects around her. The sky was now become clear and smiling; the lowring clouds were dissipated, and the blue expanse was stretched without limits over their head. The sources of her former terror were indeed removed, but the objects that presented themselves were equally alarming. All was unexpected and all was unaccountable. Imogen had remained without consciousness from the very beginning of the storm, and it was during her insensibility that the goblin had been visible, and the magician descended to the plains. She found herself mounted upon a car, and hurried along by rapid steeds. She saw beside her a man whose face, whose garb, and whose whole appearance were perfectly unknown to her.

"Ah," exclaimed the maiden, in a voice of amazement apprehension, "where am I? What is become of my Edwin? And what art thou? What means all this? These are not the well-known fields; this is not the brook of Towey, nor these hills of Clwyd. Oh, whither, whither do we fly? This track leads not to the cottage of my parents, and the groves of Rhyddlan." "Be not uneasy, my fair one," answered Roderic. "We go, though not by the usual path, to where your friends reside. I am not your enemy, but a swain who esteems it his happiness to have come between you and your distress, and to have rescued you from the pelting of the storm. Suspend, my love, for a few moments your suspicions and your anxiety, and we shall arrive where all your doubts will be removed, and all I hope will be pleasure and felicitation." While he thus spoke the chariot hastened to the conclusion of their journey, and entered the area in the front of the mansion of Roderic.

The suspicions of Imogen were indeed removed, but in a manner too cruel for her tender frame. The terror and fatigue she had previously undergone had wasted her spirits, and the surprise she now experienced, was more than she could sustain. As the chariot entered the court, she cried out with a voice of horror and anguish, and sunk breathless into the arms of her ravisher. Though the passion he had already conceived for her, made this a circumstance of affliction, he yet in another view rejoiced, that he was able, by its intervention, to conduct his prize in a manner by stealth into his palace, and thus to prevent that struggle and those painful sensations, which she must otherwise have known. For could she have borne, without emotion, to see herself conveyed into a wretched imprisonment? Could she have submitted, without opposition, to be shut up, as it were, from the hope of revisiting those scenes, where once her careless childhood played, and those friends whom she valued more than life?

The leading pursuit of Roderic, as it had been stated by the Druid of Elwy, was the love of pleasure, an attachment to sensuality, luxury and lust. He often spent whole days in the bosom of voluptuousness, reposing upon couches of down, under ceilings of gold. His senses were at intervals awakened, by the most exquisite music, to a variety of delight. He often recreated his view with beholding, from a posture of supineness and indolence, the frolic games, and the mazy dance. Sometimes, in order to diversify the scene, he would mix in the sports, and, by the graceful activity of his limbs, and the subtle keenness of his wit, would communicate relish and novelty to that which before had palled upon the performers. When he moved, every eye was fixed in admiration. When he spoke all was tranquility of attention, and every mouth was open to applaud. Then were set forth the luxuries of the feast. Every artifice was employed to provoke the appetite. The viands were savoury, and the fruits were blushing; the decorations were sumptuous, and the halls shone with a profusion of tapers, whose rays were reflected in a thousand directions by an innumerable multitude of mirrors and lustres. And now the intoxicating beverage went swiftly round the board. The conversation became more open and unrestrained. Quick were the repartees and loud the mirth. Loose, meaning glances were interchanged between the master of the feast and the mingled beauties that adorned his board. With artful inadvertence the gauze seemed to withdraw from their panting bosoms, and new and still newer charms discovered themselves to enchant the eyes and inflame the heart. The bed of enjoyment succeeded to the board of intemperance. Such was the history of the life of Roderic.

But man was not born for the indolence of pleasure and the uniformity of fruition. No gratifications, but especially not those that address themselves only to the senses, and pamper this brittle, worthless mansion of the immortal mind, are calculated to entertain us for any long duration. We need something to awaken our attention, to whet our appetite, and to contrast our joys. Happiness in this sublunary state can scarcely be felt, but by a comparison with misery. It is he only that has escaped from sickness, that is conscious of health; it is he only that has shaken off the chains of misfortune, that truly rejoices. The wisdom of these maxims was felt by Roderic. Full of pleasures, surrounded with objects of delight, he was not happy. Their uniformity cloyed him. He had received, by supernatural endowment, an activity and a venturousness of spirit, that were little formed for such scenes as these. He was devoured with spleen. He sighed he knew not why; he was peevish and ill-humoured in the midst of the most assiduous attention and the most wakeful service. And the command he possessed over the elements of nature was no remedy for sensations like these.

Oppressed with these feelings, Roderic was accustomed to withdraw himself from the pomps and luxuries that surrounded him, to fly from the gilded palace and the fretted roofs, and to mix in the simple and undebauched scenes of artless innocence that descended on every side from the hills he inhabited. The name of Roderic was unknown to all the shepherds of the vallies, and he was received by them with that officiousness and hospitality which they were accustomed to exercise to the stranger. It was his delight to give scope to his imagination by inventing a thousand artful tales of misfortune, by which he awakened the compassion, and engaged the attachment of the simple hinds. In order the more effectually to evade that curiosity which would have been fatal to his ease, he assumed every different time that he came among them a different form. By this contrivance, he passed unobserved, he partook freely of their pastimes, he made his observations unmolested, and was perfectly at leisure for the reflections, not always of the most pleasant description, that these scenes, of simple virtue and honest poverty, were calculated to excite. "Oh, impotence of power," exclaimed he, wrapt up and secure in the disguise he assumed, "to what purpose art thou desired? Ambition is surely the most foolish and misjudging of all terrestrial passions. My condition appears attractive. I am surrounded with riches and splendour; no man approaches me but with homage and flattery; every object of gratification solicits my acceptance. I am not only endowed with a capacity of obtaining all that I can wish, and that by supernatural means, but I am almost constantly forestalled in my wishes. Who would not say, that I am blessed? Who that heard but a description of my state, would not envy me? O ye shepherds, happy, thrice happy, in the confinedness of your prospects, ye would then envy me! Instructed as I am, instructed by too fatal experience, with reason I envy you. Hark to that swain who is now leading his flock from the durance in which they were held till the morning peeped over the eastern hills! The little lambs frisk about him, thankful for the liberty they have regained, and he stretches out his hand for them to lick. Now he drives them along the extended green, and in a wild and thoughtless note carols a lively lay. He sings perhaps of the kind, but bashful shepherdess. His hat is bound about with ribbon; the memorial of her coy compliance and much-prized favour. How light is his heart, how chearful his gait, and how gay his countenance! He leads in a string a little frolic goat with curving horns: I suppose the prize that he bore off in singing, which is not yet tamed to his hand, and familiarised to his flock. What though his coat be frieze? What though his labour constantly return with the returning day? I wear the attire of kings; far from labouring myself, thousands labour for my convenience. And yet he is happier than I. Envied simplicity; venerable ignorance; plenteous poverty! How gladly would I quit my sumptuous palace, and my magic arts, for the careless, airy, and unreflecting joys of rural simplicity!"

It was in a late excursion of this kind that he had beheld the beauteous Imogen. His eye was struck with the charms of her person, and the amiableness of her manners. Never had he seen a complexion so transparent, or an eye so expressive. Her vermeil-tinctured lips were new-blown roses that engrossed the sight, and seemed to solicit to be plucked. His heart was caught in the tangles of her hair. Such an unaffected bashfulness, and so modest a blush; such an harmonious and meaning tone of voice, that expressed in the softest accents, the most delicate sense and the most winning simplicity, could not but engage the attention of a swain so versed in the science of the fair as Roderic. From that distinguished moment, though he still felt uneasiness, it was no longer vacuity, it was no longer an uneasiness irrational and unaccountable. He had now an object to pursue. He was not now subjected to the fatigue of forming wishes for the sake of having them instantly gratified. When he reflected upon the present object of his desires, new obstacles continually started in his mind. Unused to encounter difficulty, he for a time imagined them insurmountable. Had his desires been less pressing, had his passion been less ardent, he would have given up the pursuit in despair. But urged along by an unintermitted impulse, he could think of nothing else, he could not abstract his attention to a foreign subject. He determined at least once again to behold the peerless maiden. He descended to the feast of Ruthyn; and though the interval had been but short, from the time in which he had first observed her, in the eye of love she seemed improved. The charms that erst had budded, were now full blown. Her beauties were ripened, and her attractions spread themselves in the face of day. Nor was this all. He beheld with a watchful glance her slight and silent intercourse with the gallant Edwin; an intercourse which no eye but that of a lover could have penetrated. Hence his mind became pregnant with all the hateful brood of dark suspicions; he was agitated with the fury of jealousy. Jealousy evermore blows the flame it seems formed to extinguish. The passion of Roderic was more violent than ever. His impatient spirit could not now brook the absence of a moment. Luxury charmed no longer; the couch of down was to him a bed of torture, and the solicitations of beauty, the taunts and sarcasms of infernal furies. He invoked the spirit of his mother; he brought together an assembly of elves and goblins. By their direction he formed his plan; by their instrumentality the tempest was immediately raised; and under the guidance of the chief of all the throng he descended upon his prey, like the eagle from his eminence in the sky.

The success of his exploit has already been related. The scheme had indeed been too deeply laid, and too artfully digested, to admit almost the possibility of a miscarriage. Who but would have stood appalled, when the storm descended upon our lovers in the midst of the plain, and the thunders seemed to rock the whole circle of the neighbouring hills? Who could have conducted himself at once with greater prudence and gallantry than the youthful shepherd? Did he not display the highest degree of heroism and address, when he laid the gaunt and haughty wolf prostrate at his feet? But it was not for human skill to cope with the opposition of infernal spirits. Accordingly Roderic had been victorious. He had borne the tender maiden unresisted from the field; he had outstripped the ardent pursuit of Edwin with a speed swifter than the winds. In fine, he had conducted his lovely prize in safety to his enchanted castle, and had introduced her within those walls, where every thing human and supernatural obeyed his nod, in a state of unresisting passivity.

Roderic, immediately upon his entrance into the castle, had committed the fair Imogen to the care of the attendant damsels. He charged them by every means to endeavour to restore her to sense and tranquility, and not to utter any thing in her hearing, which should have the smallest tendency to discompose her spirits. In obedience to orders, which they had never known what it was to dispute, they were so unwearied in their assiduities to their amiable charge, that it was not long before she began once again to exhibit the tokens of renewed perception. She raised by degrees a leaden and inexpressive eye, to the objects that were about her, without having as yet spirit and recollectedness enough to distinguish them. "My mother," cried she, "my venerable Edith, I am not well. My head is quite confused and giddy. Do press it with your friendly hand." A female attendant, as she uttered these words, drew near to obey them. "Go, go," exclaimed Imogen, with a feeble tone, and at the same time putting by the officious hand, "you naughty girl. You are not my mother. Do not think to make me believe you are."

While she spoke this she began gradually to gain a more entire sedateness and self-command. She seemed to examine, with an eager and inquisitive eye, first one object, and then another by turns. The novelty of the whole scene appeared for an instant to engross her attention. Every part of the furniture was unlike that of a shepherd's cot; and completely singular and unprecedented by any thing that her memory could suggest. But this self-deception, this abstraction from her feelings and her situation was of a continuance the shortest that can be conceived. All seemed changed with her in a moment. Her eye, which, from a state of languor and unexpressiveness, had assumed an air of intent and restless curiosity, was now full of comfortless sorrow and unprotected distress. "Powers that defend the innocent, support, guard me! Where am I? What have I been doing? What is become of me? Oh, Edwin, Edwin!" and she reclined her head upon the shoulder of the female who was nearest her.

Recovering however, in a moment, the dignity that was congenial to her, she raised herself from this remiss and inactive posture, and seemed to be immersed in reflection and thought. "Yes, yes," exclaimed she, "I know well enough how it is. You cannot imagine what a furious storm it was: and so I sunk upon the ground terrified to death: and so Edwin left me, and ran some where, I cannot tell where, for shelter. But sure it could not be so neither. He could not be so barbarous. Well but however somebody came and took me up, and so I am here. But what am I here for, and what place is this? Tell me, ye kind shepherdesses, (if shepherdesses you are) for indeed I am sick at heart."

The broken interrogatories of Imogen were heard with a profound silence. "What," said the lovely and apprehensive maiden, "will you not answer me? No, not one word. Ah, then it must be bad indeed. But I have done nothing that should make me be afraid. I am as harmless and as chearly as the little red-breast that pecks out of my hand? So you will not hurt me, will you? No, I dare swear. You do not frown upon me. Your looks are quite sweet and good-natured. But then it was not kind not to answer me, and tell me what I asked you." "Fair stranger," replied one of the throng, "we would willingly do any thing to oblige you. But you are weak and ill; and it is necessary that you should not exert yourself, but try to sleep."

"Sleep," replied the shepherdess, "what here in this strange place? No, that I shall not, I can tell you. I never slept from under the thatch of my father's cottage in my life, but once, and that was at the wedding of my dear, obliging Rovena. But perhaps," added she, "my father and mother will come to me here. So I will even try and be compliable, for I never was obstinate. But indeed my head is strangely confused; you must excuse me."

Such was the language, and such the affecting simplicity of the innocent and uncultivated Imogen. She, who had been used to one narrow round of chearful, rustic scenes, was too much perplexed to be able to judge of her situation. Her repeated faintings had weakened her spirits, and for a time disordered her understanding. She had always lived among the simple; she had scarcely ever been witness to any thing but sincerity and innocence. Suspicion therefore was the farthest in the world from being an inmate of her breast. Suspicion is the latest and most difficult lesson of the honest and uncrooked mind. Imogen therefore willingly retired to rest, in compliance with the soliciation of her attendants. She beheld no longer her ravisher, whose eye beamed with ungovernable desires, and whose crest swelled with pride. Every countenance was marked with apparent carefulness and sympathy. She was even pleased with their officious and friendly-seeming demeanour.

Tell me, ye vain cavillers, ye haughty adversaries of the omnipotence of virtue, where could artful vice, where could invisible and hell-born seduction, have found a fitter object for their triumph? Imogen was not armed with the lessons of experience: Imogen was not accoutered with the cautiousness of cultivation and refinement. She was all open to every one that approached her. She carried her heart in her hand. Ye, I doubt not, have already reckoned upon the triumph, and counted the advantages. But, if I do not much mistake the divine lessons I am commissioned to deliver, the muse shall tell a very different story.

BOOK the THIRD

PURPOSES OF RODERIC.—THE CARRIAGE

OF IMOGEN.—HER CONTEMPT OF RICHES.

T HE fatigue which Imogen had nudergone in the preceding day, prepared
her to rest during the night with more tranquility than could otherwise have
been expected. The scenes to which she had successively been witness, and the
objects that now surrounded her, were too novel and extraordinary in their character, to allow much room for the severity of reflection, and the coolness of meditation. Her frame was tired with the various exercises in which she had engaged;
her mind was hurried and perplexed without knowing upon what to fix, or in what
manner to account for the events that had befallen her: she therefore sunk presently into a sweet and profound sleep; and while every thing seemed preparing
for her destruction, while a thousand enchantments were essayed, and a thousand
schemes revolved in the busy mind of Roderic, she remained composed and unapprehensive. Innocence was the sevenfold shield that protected her from harm;
her eyes were closed in darkness, and a smile of placid benignity played upon the
lovely features of her countenance.

Roderic in the mean time had retired to his chamber. His mind was turbid and
unquiet. So restless are the waves of the ocean before the coming tempest. They
assume a darker hue, and reflect a more cloudy heaven. They roll this way and
that in a continual motion, and yet without any direction, till the loud and hoarse-
echoing wind determines their course and carries them in mountains to the sounding shore. The mind of the victim was all quiet and unruffled; such is the kindly
influence of conscious truth. The mind of the ravisher exhibited nothing but
uneasiness and confusion; such are the boons which vice bestows upon her misjudging votaries.

The conqueror, doubly misled by fierce and unruly passions and by his inauspicious commerce with the goblins of the abyss, retired not immediately to his
couch, but walked up and down his apartments, with a hasty and irregular step.
"Thanks to my favourable stars," exclaimed he, "I am triumphant! What power
can resist me? Where is the being that shall dare to say, that one wish of my heart
shall go unfulfilled? Well then, I have got the fair the charming she into my power.
She is shut up in a palace, unseen by every human eye, to which no human foot
ever found its way but at my bidding. She is closed round with spells and enchantment. I can by a word deprive her every limb of motion. If I but wave this wand,
the leaden God of sleep shall sink her in a moment in the arms of forgetfulness,
whatever were before her anxieties and her wakeful terrors. In what manner
then shall I, thus absolute and uncontroled in all I bid exist, proceed? Shall I
press the unwilling beauty to my bosom, and riot in her hoard of charms, without
waiting like meaner mortals to sue for the consent of her will? There is something
noble, royal, and independent, in the thought. Beauty never appears so attrac-

tive as from behind a veil of tears. Oh, how I enjoy infancy [sic] the anger that shall flush her lovely cheek! Perhaps she will even kneel to me to deprecate that which an education of prejudices has taught her to consider as the worst of evils. Yes, my lovely maid, I will raise thee. Do not turn from me those scornful indignant eyes. I will be thy best friend. I will not hurt a hair of thy head. Oh, when her spotless bosom pants with disdain, how sweet to beat the little chiders, and by a friendly violence, which true and comprehensive wisdom cannot stigmatize, to teach her what is the true value of beauty, and for what purpose such enchanting forms as her's were sent to dwell below!"

Thus spoke the ravisher, and as he spoke he assumed, although alone, a firmer stride and a more haughty crest. Upon the instant however his ears were saluted with a low and continual sound, that became, by just degrees, stronger and more strong. The walls of his palace shook; a sudden and supernatural light gleamed along his apartment, and a spectre stood before him. Roderic lifted up his eyes, and immediately recognised the features of that goblin, who from the hour of his birth, had declared himself his adversary. He had been repeatedly used to the visits of this malicious spirit, who delighted to subvert all his schemes, and to baffle his deepest projects. This was the only misfortune, the sovereign of the hills had ever known; this was the only instance in which he had at any time been taught what it was to have his power controled and his nod unobeyed. He had often sought, by means of the confederacy he held with other spirits of the infernal regions, to restrain his enemy, or by punishment and suffering to make him rue his opposition. But the goblin he had to encounter, though not the most potent, was of all the rest the most crafty in his wiles, and the most abundant in expedients. As many times as his fellows had by the instigation of Roderic undertaken to encounter him, so often had they in the end been eluded and defeated. The contest was now given up, and the goblin was at liberty to haunt and threaten his impotant adversary as much as he pleased.

"Roderic," cried he, with a harsh and unpleasant accent, "I am come to humble the haughtiness of thy triumph, and to pull down thy aspiring thoughts. Impotent and rancorous mortal! Know, that innocence is defended with too strong a shield for thee to pierce! Boast not thyself of the immensity of thy walls, and put no confidence in the subtlety of thy enchantments. Before the mightiness that waits on innocence, they are not less impotent than the liquid wax, or the crumbling ruin. Learn, oh presumptuous mortal, that sacred and unyielding chastity is invulnerable to all the violence of men, and all the stratagems of goblins. I would not name to thee so salutary an advice as to dismiss thy innocent and unsuspicious prize, did not I know thee too obstinate and headstrong to listen to the voice of wisdom. Essay then thy base and low-minded temptations, thy corrupt and sophistical reasonings, to tarnish the unsullied purity of her mind, and it is well. If by such a wretch as thee she can be seduced from the obedience of virtue and the Gods, then let her fall. She were then a victim worthy of thee. But if thou essayest the means of tyranny and force, the attempt will be fatal to thee. I will in that case enjoy my vengeance; I will triumph in thy desolation. In the hour then of action and enterprise, remember me!"

With these words the spectre vanished from his sight. Roderic was inflamed with anger and disgust; but he had none, upon whom to wreak his revenge. His heart boiled with the impotence of malice. "What," cried he, "am I to be bounded and hedged in, in all my exploits? Am I to be curbed and thwarted in every wish of my heart? This, this was nearest to me. This was the first pursuit of my life in which my whole heart was engaged; the first time I ever felt a passion that deserved the name of love. But be it so: I was born with wild and impetuous passions only to have them frustrated; I was endowed with supernatural powers, and inherited all my mother's skill, only to be the more signally disappointed. Still however I will not shrink, I will not yield an inch to my adversary. I am bid, it seems, to tempt her, and endeavour to stain the purity of her mind. Yes, I will tempt her. It is not for an artless and uninstructed shepherdess to defeat my wiles and baffle all my incitements. I will dazzle her senses with all the attractions that the globe of earth has to boast. I will wind me into her secret heart. Thou damned, unpropitious goblin, who seekest to oppose thyself to my happiness, I will but, by thy warning, gain a completer triumph! I will subdue her will. She shall crown my wishes with ripe, consenting beauty. Long shall she remain the empress of my heart, and partner of my bed. In her I will hope to find those simple, artless, and engaging charms, which in vain I have often sought in the band of females, that reside beneath my roof, and wait upon my nod."

Imogen, though considerably indisposed by the fatigue and terrors of the preceding day, shook off however that placid and refreshing sleep which had weighed down her eyelids, long before Roderic deserted the couch of luxury. Two of the female attendants belonging to the castle had slept in the same apartment with her, and soon, perceiving her in motion, followed her example, and officiously pressed around her. One of them took up a part of the garb of the fair shepherdess, and offered to assist her in adjusting it. "I thank you," cried Imogen, with the utmost simplicity, "for your good-nature; but I am pretty well now; and every body dresses herself that is not sick." The inartificial decorations of her person were quickly adjusted. The delicate proportion of her limbs was hid beneath a russet mantle; her fair and flowing tresses were disposed in a braid round her head, and she took her straw hat in her hand. "Well," said she, "I am obliged to you for your favours. I dare say it was best for me, though at the time I thought otherwise. For my head ached very much, and I was so weak — It was wrong for me to think of going any farther. — Ah, but then, what have my poor father and mother done all the while? Have not they missed their Imogen, and wondered what was become of her, and been quite sad and forlorn for fear she should have come to any harm? Well, I do not know whether I was not right too. For their ease was of more consequence than mine. I cannot tell. However I will not now keep them in pain. So good morning to you, my dear kind friends!" And saying this she was tripping away.

But as she drew towards the door, one of the attendants, with a gentle force, took hold of her hand. "Do not go yet, sweet Imogen," cried she. "We want a little more of your company. We have done you all the service in our power, and you have not paid us for it. We will not ask any thing hard and unreasonable of you.

Only comply with us in this one thing, to stay with us a few hours, and let us know a little better the worth of that amiable female we have endeavoured to oblige." "Indeed, indeed," replied Imogen, "I cannot. I am not used to be obstinate; and you are so kind and fair spoken, that it goes to my heart to refuse you. But I would not for the world keep my dear, good Edith in a moment's suspense. But since you are so desirous of being acquainted with me, repair as soon and as often as you please to my father's cot, that lies on the right hand side of the valley, about a mile from the sea, and just beside the pretty brawling brook of Towey. There I will treat you with the nicest apples and the richest cream. And I would treat you with better, if I knew of any thing better, that I might thank you for your goodness. Farewell!" added she, and affectionately pressed the hand that was still untwined with her's.

"No, Imogen, no, you must not leave us thus. Though we would have done a thousand times more than we have for your own sake, who are so simple and so good, it is yet fit that you should know, that we are not mistresses here, and that all we have done has been by the orders of the lord of this rich mansion. He will not therefore forgive us, if we suffer you to depart before he has seen you, and expressed for you that kindness which induced him to take you under his protection." "Heavens!" replied the shepherdess "this is all ceremony and folly, and therefore cannot be of so much consequence as the peace of my father, and the consolation of my mother. Tell him, that I thank him, and that my father shall thank him too, if he will come to our hut. Tell him that I am sorry for my foolish weakness, that gave him so much trouble, and made me be so needlessly frightened, when we came to a place where I have met with nothing but kindness; but I could not help it. And so that is enough; for if my Edwin had been in his place, and had seen a stranger shepherdess in the distress that I was, he would surely have done as much.

"Say so to your lord, as you call him, for I would not seem ungrateful. But yet I will thank you a great deal more than I do him. For what did he do for me? He took me, and hurried me away, and paid no attention to my tears and expostulations. Well, but I need not have been alarmed. So it seems. But I did not like his looks; they were not kind and good-natured, but fierce and frightful. And so as soon as he had brought me here, much against my will, he went away and left me. So much the better. And then you came and took care of me, and he desired you to do so. That was well enough. But I am more obliged to you for your kindness and assiduity, than I am to him only for thinking of it. And then to tell you the truth, but I ought not to say so to you who are his friends, there is something about him, I cannot tell what, that does not please me at all. He looks discontented, and fierce, as if there was no such thing as soothing and managing him. But why do I say all this? Pray now let me go, let me go to my dear, dear mother."

"Sweet Imogen," replied the attendant, who seemed to take the lead in the circle, "how lovely and amiable are you even in your resentments! They are not with you a morose and gloomy sullenness brooding over imaginary wrongs, and collecting venom and malice from every corner to the heart. In your breast anger itself takes a milder form, and is gentle, generous and gay. Yet why, my Imogen, should you harbour any anger against your protector?

Such was the honest and artless dialogue of Imogen. The attendants rather endeavoured to beguile the time, by dexterously starting new topics of conversation, upon which Imogen delivered her plain and natural sentiments with the utmost sincerity, than to detain her by open force. At length one of them slipped out, and hastened to acquaint Roderic with the impatience of his prize, and to communicate to him the substance of those artless hints, which, in the hands of so skilful and potent an impostor, might be of the greatest service. Roderic immediately rose. But as he was desirous to decorate his person with the nicest skill, in order to make the most favourable impression upon his mistress, he ordered the attendant, with some of her companions, to wait upon Imogen. He commissioned them, if it were necessary, to inform her of the absolute impossibility of her quitting the castle, and to persuade her to walk in the meadows adjoining, that she might observe the riches of their possessor; how fertile were the soil, and how fair and numerous the flocks.

The patience of Imogen, in the mean time, was nearly exhausted. Her simplicity could no longer be duped. Though unused to art, it was imposssible for her not at length to perceive the art by which the conversation was lengthened, and her ardent desire to set out for the cottage of her father, eluded. She was just beginning to expostulate upon this ungenerous stratagem, when three or four of those females, whom Roderic had dispatched entered the apartment. "Well," cried Imogen, "you have borne my message to my deliverer, now then let me go." "Our lord," replied the attendant, "is just risen. He will but adjust his apparel, and will immediately pay you those respects in person which he can by no means think of omitting." "Alas, alas," cried the shepherdess, half distressed, "what is the meaning of all this? What is intended by a language so foreign to the homeliness of the shepherd's cot, and the admirable simplicity of pastoral life? I know not what title I have, a poor, unpretending virgin, to the respects of this lord; but surely if they meaned me well, they would be less hollow and absurd. Would there not be much more respect, much more civility, in permitting me to follow my own inclinations, without this arbitrary and ungrateful restraint?" "Shepherdess," replied the attendant, "we are not used to dispute the orders of our master. We would oblige you if it were in our power. Impute not therefore to us any thing unfriendly; and as for Roderic, he is too good, and too amiable, not to be able to satisfy you about his conduct the moment he appears." "Your master! and your lord!" replied Imogen, with a tone of displeasure, "I understand not these words. The Gods have made all their rational creatures equal. If they have made one strong and another weak, it is for the purpose of mutual benevolence and assistance, and not for that of despotism and oppression. Of all the shepherds of the valley, there is not one that claims dominion and command over another. There is indeed an obedience due from children to their parents, and from a wife to her husband. But ye cannot be his children; for he is young and blooming. And but one of you can be his wife; so that that cannot be the source of his authority. What a numerous family has this Roderic? Does that I wonder, make him happier than his fellows?"

"Imogen," said one of the train, "will you walk with us along the meadow, by the side of that hazel copse? The morning is delightful, the sun shines with a mild and cheering heat, the lambs frisk along the level green, and the birds, with their little throats, warble each a different strain." The mind of Imogen was highly susceptible to the impression of rural beauties. She had that placid innocence, that sweet serenity of heart, which best prepares us to relish them. Seeing therefore, that she was a prisoner, and that it was in vain to struggle and beat her wings against the wiry inclosure, she submitted. "Ah! unjust, unkind associates!" exclaimed Imogen, "ye can obey the dictates of a man, who has no right to your obedience, and ye can turn a deaf ear to the voice of benevolence and justice! Set me at liberty. This man has no right to see me, and I will not see him. I, that have been used to wander as free as the inmates of the wood, or the winged inhabitants of air, shall I be cooped up in a petty cage, have all my motions dictated, and all my walks circumscribed? Indeed, indeed, I will not. Imogen can never submit to so ignominious a restraint. She will sooner die."

"Why, my lovely maiden," replied the other, "will you think so harshly of our lord? He does not deserve these uncandid constructions; he is all gentleness and goodness. Suspend therefore your impatience for a moment. By and by you may represent to him your uneasiness, and he will grant you all the wishes of your heart. Till then, amiable girl, compose your spirits, and give us cause to believe, that you place that confidence in us, which for the world we would not deserve to forfeit."

During this conversation, they passed along a gallery, and, descending by a flight of stairs, proceeded through one corner of a spacious garden into the meadow. The mansion, as we have already said, stood upon a rising ground, which was inclosed on every side by a circle of hills, whose summits seemed to touch the clouds, and were covered with eternal snow. Within this wider circumference was a second formed by an impervious grove of oaks, which, though of no long standing, yet, having been produced by magical art, had appeared from the first in full maturity. Their vast trunks, which three men hand in hand could scarcely span, were marked with many a scar, and their broad branches, waving to the winds, inspired into the pious and the virtuous that religious awe, which is one of the principal lessons of the Druidical religion.

At no great distance, and close on one side to the majestic grove, was a terrace, raised by the hand of art, so elevated, as to overlook the tops of the trees as well as the turrets of the castle, and to afford a complete prospect of all the grounds on this side the precipices. To this terrace the attendants of Imogen led their charge, and from it she surveyed the farms and granges of their lord. The view was diversified by a number of little rills, that flowed down from the mountains, and gave fertility and cheerfulness to the fields through which they passed. The inclosures were some of them covered with a fine and rich herbage, whose appearance was bright and verdant, and its surface besprinkled with cowslips, king-cups, and daisies. Others of them were interspersed with sheep that exhibited the face of sleekness and ease, their fleeces large and ponderous, and their wool of the finest and most admirable texture. Elsewhere you might see the cattle grazing. The ox dappled with a thousand spots, which nature seemed to have applied with a wanton and playful hand; the cow, whose udders were distended with milk, that appeared to call for the interposition of the maidens to lighten them of their store; and the lordly and majestic bull. With them was intermingled the horse, whose limbs seemed to be formed for speed and beauty. At a small distance were the stag with branching horns, the timid deer, and the sportive, frisking fawn. Even from the rugged precipices, that seemed intended by nature to lie waste and useless, depended the shaggy goat and the tender kid. Beside all this, Roderic had had communicated to him, by a supernatural afflatus, that wondrous art, as yet unknown in the plains of Albion, of turning up the soil with a share of iron, and scattering it with a small quantity of those grains which are most useful to man, to expect to gather, after a short interval, a forty-fold increase.

Every thing conspired to communicate to the prospect lustre and attraction. The birds, with their various song, gave an air of populousness and animation to the grove. By the side of the rivulets were scattered here and there the huts of the shepherd and husbandman. And though these swains were not, like the happy dwellers in the valley, enlivened with freedom, and made careless and gay by conscious innocence; yet were they skilful to give clearness and melody to the slender reed; and the ploughman whistled as he drove afield. But that in the land-scape which most engrossed the attention and awakened the curiosity of the tender Imogen, was the appearance of the fields of corn. It was in her eye novel, agreeable, and interesting. The harvest was near, and the effect of the object was at its greatest height. The tall and unbending stalk overtopped by far the native herbage of the meadow, and seemed to emulate the hawthorn and the hazel, which, planted in even rows, secured the precious crop from the invasion of the cattle. The ears were embrowned with the continual beams of the sun, and, oppressed with the weight of their grain, bended from the stalk. In a word, the whole pre-sented to the astonished view a rich scene of vegetable gold. Upon this delightful object the shepherdess gazed with an unwearied regard. Respecting it she asked innumerable questions, and made a thousand enquiries; and it almost seemed as if her curiosity would never be satisfied. Such is the power of novelty over the young and inexperienced, and such the influence of the beautiful and transcendent beau-ties of nature upon the ingenuous and uncorrupted mind. But it was not possible for the shepherdess, interested as she was in the uneasiness, to which she knew that her parents must be a prey, long to banish from her mind the affecting consideration, or to divert her attention to another object, however agreeable, or however fascinating.

She had just begun to renew her representations upon this head, when Roderic approached. While he was yet at a distance, he appeared graceful and gay, as the messenger of the God that grasps the lightning in his hand. His stature was above the common size. His limbs were formed with perfect symmetry; the fall of his shoulders was graceful, and the whole contour of his body was regular and pleasing. Such was the general effect of his shape, that though his advance was hesitating and respectful, it was impossible to contemplate his person without the ideas being suggested of velocity and swiftness. His presence and air had the appearance of frankness, ingenuousness, and manly confidence. The natural fire and haughtiness of his eye were carefully subdued, and he seemed, at least to a superficial view, the very model of good-nature and disinterested complaisance. His bright and flowing hair parted on his brow, and formed into a thousand ringlets, waved to the zephyrs as he passed along. There was something so delicate and enchanting in his whole figure, as to tempt you to compare it to the unspotted beauty of the hyacinth; at the same time that you rejoiced, that it was not a beauty, frail and transient, as the tender flower, but which promised a manly ripeness and a protracted duration.

Observing that the attention of those around her was suddenly diverted from the intreaties she employed, Imogen turned her eye, in order to discover the object that now engaged them. It was immediately met by the graceful and amiable figure we have described. But to Imogen that figure presented no such comeliness and beauty. For a moment indeed, nature prevailed, and she could not avoid gazing, with a degree of complacence, upon an object, to which the Goddess seemed to have lavished all her treasures. But this sensation vanished, almost before it was formed. The mind of the shepherdess was too deeply read in the lessons of virtue, to acknowledge any beauty in that form, which was not animated with truth, and in those features, which were not illuminated with integrity and innocence. Notwithstanding her native simplicity, and the unsuspecting confidence she was inclined to repose in every individual of the human race, yet had the conduct of Roderic, as she had already confessed, displeased her too deeply for her immediately to assume towards him an unembarrassed and soothing carriage. He had seized upon her by violence in a moment of insensibility. He had carried her away without her consent. When she recovered strength enough to expostulate upon this, he endeavoured, by ambiguous expressions, to deceive her into an opinion, that he was conducting her to the cottage of her father. Supposing that, for reasons good and wise, he had introduced her into a strange place, she could not be persuaded that those reasons subsisted for detaining her contrary to her inclination. And independently of any individual circumstances, there is a native and inexplicable antipathy between virtue and vice. It is not in the nature of things, it is not within the range of possibility, that they should coalesce and unite where both of them exist in a decided manner, or an eminent degree. It was not the babble of ignorance, it was by an unalterable law of her nature, that Imogen had been displeased with the looks of him, who meaned her destruction. The animation that dwells in the features of virtue, is mild and friendly and lambent; but the sparkles that flash from the eye of enterprising guilt, are momentary, and unrelenting, and impetuous. The gentle and the inoffensive instantly feel how uncongenial they are to their dispositions, and start back from them with aversion and horror. Such were in some measure the sensations of Imogen, upon the re-appearance of her betrayer. She turned from him with unfeigned dislike, and was reluctantly kept in the same situation till he ascended the terrace.

As he drew nearer, Roderic seized the hand of the lovely captive. In a tone of blandishment he expostulated with her upon her unkind behaviour and unreasonable aversion. With all that sophistry, that ingenious vice knows so well how to employ, he endeavoured to evince that his conduct had been regulated by kindness, rectitude and humanity. In the mean time the retinue withdrew to a small distance. Imogen insisted upon not being left wholly alone with her ravisher.

Able to perplex but not to subvert the understanding of his prize, Roderic addressed her with the language of love. Naturally eloquent, all that he now said was accompanied with that ineffable sweetness, and that soft insinuation, that must have shaken the integrity of Imogen, had her heart been less constant, and her bosom less glowed with the enthusiasm of virtue. Her betrayer was conscious to a real, though a degenerate flame, and was not reduced to feign an ardour he did not feel. Recollecting however the pure manners, and the delicate and ingenuous language to which Imogen had been inured among the inhabitants of Clwyd, the subtle sorcerer did not permit an expression to escape him, that could offend the chastest ear, or alarm the most suspicious virtue. His love, ardent as it appeared, seemed to be entirely under the government of the strictest propriety, and the most unfeigned rectitude. He knew that the inspirations of integrity and the lessons of education were not to be eradicated at once; and he attempted not to gain the acquiescence of his captive by gross and unsuitable allurements, unconcealed with the gilding of dexterity and speciousness.

But his eloquence and his address were equally vain. In spite of the beauty of his person and the urbanity of his manners, the shepherdess received his declarations with coldness and aversion. She assured him of the impossibility of his success, that she felt for him emotions very different from those of partiality, and that her heart was prepossessed for a more amiable swain. With that sweet simplicity, that accompanied all she did, she endeavoured to dissuade him from the pursuit of a hopeless and unreasonable passion; she enumerated to him all the sources of enjoyment with which he was surrounded; she intreated him not in the wantonness of opulence to disturb her humble and narrow felicity; and she besought him in the most pathetic and earnest language to dismiss her to freedom, contentment and her parents.

The more she exerted herself to bend his resolution, and the more scope she gave to the unstudied expression of her artless sentiments, the more inextricably was the magician caught, and the more firm and inexorable was his purpose. Perceiving however that he had little to hope from the most skilful detail of the pleas of passion, he turned the attention of the shepherdess to a different topic. "Behold Imogen," cried he, "the richness of the landscape on our right hand! The spot in my eye is farthest from the castle, and divided from the rest of the prospect with a tall hedge of poplars and alders. It is full of the finest grass, and its soil is rich and luxuriant. It is scattered with fleckered cows and dappled fawns. In the hither part of it is a field of the choicest wheat, whose stalks are so rank and pregnant, that the timid hare and the untamed fox can scarcely force themselves a path among them. Beside it is an inclosure of barley with strong and pointed spikes; and another of oats, whose grain, uneared, spreads broader to the eye. How beautiful the scene! I will not ask you, fairest of your sex, to give your confidence to unauthorised words. I will afford the most unquestionable demonstration of the veracity of my declarations. All these, lovely Imogen, shall be yours: yours exclusively, to be disposed of at your pleasure, without the interference or control of any. All my other possessions shall not belong to myself more than to you. You shall be the mistress of my heart, and the associate of my counsels. All my business shall be your gratification, all my pleasure your happiness. Forget then, dearest maiden, the poverty of your former condition, and the connections you formed in an hour of ignorance and obscurity. From this moment let a new æra and better prospects commence. Enjoy that wealth, which can no where so well be bestowed; and those gratifications, which so obviously belong to that delicate and enchanting form."

The proposal of Roderic called forth more than ever the spirit and the resentment of Imogen. She did not feel herself in the slightest degree attracted by the magnificence of his offers. She knew of no use for superfluous riches. She felt no wants unsupplied, and no wishes ungratified. What motive is there in the whole region of human perceptions, that can excite the contented mind to the pursuit of affluence? "And dost thou think," said the fair one, with a gesture of disdain that made her look ten times more amiable, "to seduce me with baits like these? Know, mistaken man, that I am happy. I spin the finest wool of our flocks, and drain the distended udders of our cows. I superintend the dairies; the butter and the cheese are the produce of my industry. In these employments my time is spent in chearfulness and pleasure. Surrounded with our little possessions, I am conscious to no deficiency; in the midst of my parents and friends, I desire not to look beyond the narrow circle of the neighbouring hills. If you feel those wants, which I do not so much as understand, enjoy your fond mistake. Possess those riches which I will not envy you. Wander from luxury to luxury unquestioned; I shall be sufficiently happy in the narrow gratifications that nature has placed within my reach. The gifts you offer me have no splendour in my eye, and I could not thank you for them though offered with ever so much disinterestedness. The only gift it is in your power to make is liberty. Allow me to partake of that bounty, which nature has bestowed upon the choristers of the grove, to wander where I will. Under a thousand of those privations that would render the child of luxury inconsolable, I would support myself; freedom and independence are the only boons which the whole course of my life has taught me to cherish."

"Your ignorance," rejoined Roderic, "is amiable, though unfortunate. But your merit is too great not to deserve to be informed. Knowledge, my lovely maiden, is always regarded as a desirable acquisition by the prudent and the judicious. To what purpose was a mind so capacious, competent to the greatest improvements, and formed to comprehend subjects of the most extensive compass, or the sublimest reach, bestowed upon us, if it be not employed in the pursuits of science and experience? Your abilities, my Imogen, appear to be of the very first description. How much then will you be to be blamed, if you do not embrace this opportunity of improvement and instruction? Beauty, though unseen, is not less excellent; and prudence, though unpossessed, is of value inestimable. The poor man may be contented, because he knows not the use of riches; but, in spite of this contentment, it were wise to enlarge our sphere of sensation, and to extend the sources of happiness.

"If however you still maintain that lovely perverseness, decide if you please upon your own fate, but let filial piety hinder you from determining too hastily respecting that of your parents and your friends. Consider what a new and un-bounded scope will be afforded you, by the participation of my riches, for the exercise of benevolent and generous propensities. Your parents are now declining fast under the weight of years and infirmity. It is in your power to make their bed of down, and to enliven the ground they have yet to traverse with flowers. It is yours to wrest the sheers from the hand of the weary and over-laboured antient, and to remove the distaff from the knees of your venerable mother. Think, gentle shepherdess, before it be too late, of the heart-felt pleasures that await the power to do good, when attended with a virtuous inclination. When you wipe away the tear from the cheek of distress, when you light up a smile in the eye of misery, think you, that none of the comfort you administer will flow back in generous and refreshing streams to your own heart? Are these exertions that Imogen ought to contemplate with indifference? Is this a power that Imogen can reject without deliberation?"

Imogen stood for a moment in a sweet and ingenuous state of suspense. She had a native and indefeasible reverence for every thing that had the remotest analogy to virtue, and she could not answer a proposal that came recommended to her by that name with unhesitating promptitude. She was too good and modest to assume an air of decision where she did not feel it; she was too simple and unaffected, to disguise that hesitation to which she was really conscious. "How false and treach-erous," exclaimed she, "are your reasonings! Among the virtuous inhabitants of the plain, every one seeks to influence another by motives which are of weight with himself, and utters the sentiments of his own heart. Where have you learned the disingenuous and faithless arts you employ? To what purpose have you culti-vated them, and whose good opinion do you flatter yourself they will obtain for you? False, perfidious Roderic! the more I see of you, the more I fear and despise you.

"You would recommend to me your temptations under the colour of knowlege. Has knowlege any charms for the debauched and luxurious? You tell me we ought to enlarge our sphere of sensation, and to extend the sources of happiness. Wisdom indeed, and mental improvements are desirable. But the sage Druids have always taught me, that the mind is the nobler part, that the body is to be kept in subjec-tion, and that it is not our business to seek its gratification beyond the bounds of necessity and temperance. If I allowed myself to think that I wanted more than I have, might not the possession of that more extend my desires, till, from humble and bounded, they became insatiable? Were I to dismiss those industrious pursuits by means of which my time now glides so pleasantly, how am I sure that indolence and vacancy would make me happier?

"To succour indeed the necessitous, and particularly my parents and relations, is a consideration of more value. But ah, Roderic! though you talk it so well, I am afraid it is a consideration foreign to your character. For my parents, they are as yet healthful and active; and while they continue so, they wish, no more than myself for repose and indolence. If ever they become incapable of industry, their

little flock will still contribute to their support. They are too much respected, for
the neighbouring shepherds not to watch over it in turn out of pure love. And,
I hope, as I will then exert myself with double vigour, that the Gods will bless us,
and we shall do very well. As to general distress, heaven is too propitious to us,
to permit the inhabitants of the valley to be overwhelmed by it. And I shall always
have milk from my flocks, and a cheese from my store, to set before the hungry
and necessitous.

"But were these advantages more valuable than they are, it would not be my
duty to purchase them so dear. What, shall I desert all the connections it has
been the business of my life to form, and that happy state of simplicity I love so
much? Shall I shake off the mutual vows I have exchanged with the most amiable
and generous of the swains, and join myself to one, whose person I cannot love,
and whose character I cannot approve? No, Roderic, enjoy that happiness, if it
deserve the name of happiness, that is congenial to your inclination. Forget the
worthless and unreasonable passion, you pretend to have conceived, in the multitude of gratifications that are within your reach. Envy not me my straw-defended
roof, my little flock, and my faithful shepherd. I will never exchange them for
all the temptations that the world can furnish."

BOOK the FOURTH

SONG IN HONOUR OF THE FAIR SEX.—HYPOCRISY OF THE MAGICIAN.—
THE TRIUMPH OF IMOGEN.—DESPAIR AND CONSOLATION OF RODERIC.

So much was Roderic discouraged by the apparent spirit and firmness of these declarations, that at the conclusion of them he abruptly quitted his captive, and released her for a moment from his unjust persecutions. His pride however was too strongly piqued, and his passions too much alarmed to permit her a real respite. "Where ever," cried he, as he trod with hasty and irregular steps the level green, — "where ever were found such simplicity, and so much strength of judgment, and gaiety of wit in union? Is it possible for the extreme of simplicity and the perfection of intellect to meet together? These surely are paradoxes, that not all the goblins of the abyss can solve, and which, had they been related instead of seen, must have appeared to constitute an absurd and impossible fiction.

"Well then it is in vain to attack the inexorable fair one with allurements that address themselves only to the understanding. She is too well fortified with the prejudices of education, and the principles of an imaginary virtue, to be reduced by an assault like this. The pride of her virtue is alarmed, the little train of her sophistries are awakened, and with that artless rhetoric, of the value of which she is doubtless sensible, she set[s] all her enemies at defiance. My future enticements shall therefore address themselves to her senses. Thus approaching her, it is impossible that success should not follow my undertaking. Even the most wary, circumspect, and suspicious, might thus be overcome. But she is innocence itself. She apprehends no danger, she suspects no ambuscade. Young and unexperienced, and the little experience she has attained, derived only from scenes of pastoral simplicity, she knows not the meaning of insincerity and treachery; she dreads not the serpent that lurks beneath the flower."

Having determined the plan of his machinations, and given the necessary orders, he privately signified to the attendants, that they should propose to their lovely charge to direct her course once again to the mansion; and as she perceived that Roderic still continued upon a distant part of the lawn; and as she saw no means of present escape from her confinement, she consented to do as they desired.

They now entered the mansion, and passing through several splendid apartments, at length reached a large and magnificent saloon. It was hung with tapestry, upon which were represented the figures of Sappho sweeping the lyre; of the Spartan mother bending over the body, and counting the wounds of her son; of Penelope in the midst of her maidens, carefully unravelling the funeral web of her husband; of Lucretia inflicting upon herself a glorious and voluntary death; and of Arria teaching her husband in what manner a Roman should expire. These stories had been miraculously communicated to Roderic, and were now explained by the attendants to the wondering Imogen. At the same time a band of music, that was placed at the lower end of the hall, struck at once their various instruments, and, without any previous preparation, began the lofty chorus. At the upper end of the saloon stood a throne of ivory, hung round with trappings of gold, and placed upon a floor of marble, of which a numerous flight of steps, also of marble, composed the ascent. The hangings were of crimson velvet, and the canopy of the richest purple. With the musicians were intermingled a number of supernatural beings under the command of Roderic. Their voices were melodious beyond all example of human power; they were by turns lofty and majestic, and by turns tender and melting; and the strain was divine.

"Such are the honours of the tender sex; and who can speak their praise? The lily is not so fair, the rose is not so attractive, the violet and the jessamine have not so elegant a simplicity. By their charms, by their eloquence, and by their merit, they have assumed an empire over the bolder sex. How auspicious is the empire! They hold them in silken chains. They govern, not by harsh decrees, and rigorous penalties; but by smiles and soft compliances, and winning, irresistible persuasion. The rewards they bestow are sweet, and ravishing, and indescribable.

"What were man without the fair? A wild beast of the forest; a rough and untamed savage; a hungry lion bursting from his den. Without them, they are gloomy, morose, unfeeling, and unsociable. To them they owe every civilization, and every improvement. Did Amphion, from the rude and shapeless stones, raise by his power a regular edifice, houses, palaces, and cities? Did Orpheus by his lay humanize the rugged beasts and teach the forests to listen? No, these are wild, unmeaning fables. It was woman, charming woman, that led unpolished man forth from the forests and the dens, and taught him to bend before thy shrine, humanity! See how the face of nature changes! Where late the slough mantled, or the serpent hissed among the briars and the reeds, all is pasture and fertility. The cottages arise. The shepherds assume the guise of gentleness and simplicity. They attire themselves with care, they braid the garland, and they tune the pipe. Wherefore do they braid the garland? Why are their manners soft and blandishing? And why do the hills re-echo the notes of the slender reed? It is to win thy graces, woman, charming woman!

"When nature formed a man, she formed a creature rational, and erect; ten times more noble than the birds of the air, and the beasts of the field. But when she formed a woman — it was then first, that she outdid herself, and improved her own design. What are the broad and nervous shoulders, what the compacted figure, and the vigorous step, when contrasted with the well-turned limbs, the slender waist, the graceful shoulders, and the soft and panting bosom? What are the manly front, the stern, commanding eye, and the down-clad cheek, if we compare them with the smooth, transparent complexion, the soft, faint blushes, and the pretty, dimpled mouth? What are the strong, slow reason, the deep, unfathomed science, and the grave and solemn wisdom, if they are brought into competition with the sprightly sense, the penetrating wit, and the inexhaustible invention? Does the stronger sex boast of its learning, its deep researches, its sagacious discoveries? and have they a coolness, a self-command, a never baffled prudence like that which woman has exhibited? Do they pique themselves upon their courage, their gallantry, and their adventure? Where shall we find among them a patience, a mildness, a fortitude, a heroism, equal to that of the fair?

"Virtue has dwelt beneath the sun. Themis has left her throne on the right hand of Jove, and descended to the globe of earth. We have seen examples of disinterested rectitude, of inviolable truth, of sublime and heaven-born benevolence. They are written in the roll of fame; they are handed down from age to age. They are the song of the poet, and the favourite theme of the servants of the Gods. By whom were they exhibited, or with whom did they originate? With woman, charming woman? Well have justice and rectitude been represented under a female form, for without the softer sex, all had been anarchy and confusion; every man had preyed upon his neighbour; men, like beasts, had devoured each other, and virtue fled affrighted to her native skies. This is the source of all that is good and all that is excellent; of all that is beautiful and all that is sublime: woman, charming woman!"

At this place the chorus ceased for a moment, and the attendants observing, that Imogen was standing, intreated her to seat herself. She was rendered weak and languid by the unexperienced anxieties and terrors she had undergone, and she did not refuse their request. There was no seat in the centre of the hall, or nearer than the sumptuous throne that was placed at the upper end. Thither therefore they led her. Imogen had been unused to the distinctions of rank and precedence. Among the shepherds of the valley, every one, except the bards and the priests, seated himself promiscuously; none sought to take the upper hand of his neighbour; age was not distinguished by priority of place; and youth thought not of ceding the *pas*. The shepherdess, as she advanced towards the chair, paused for an instant, impressed with that blaze of magnificence which is equally formed to strike every human eye. She looked round her with an air of timidity and suspense, and then going forward, ascended the steps and placed herself in the throne. At this action, as at a signal, the song recommenced.

"Simplicity, child of nature, daughter of the plains, with thee alone the queen of beauty dwells! What is it that adorns and enhances all the wild and uncultivated scenes of nature? It is plainness and artless simplicity. What is it that renders lovely and amiable her most favourite productions in the animal creation: the tender lamb, the cooing dove, and the vocal nightingale? It is simplicity; it is, that all their gestures wear the guise, and their voice speaks the artless, and unaffected language of nature. What is is that renders venerable the characters of mankind; that ennobles the song of the bards; that gives lustre and attraction to immortal, never-fading virtue? It is simplicity, unaffected simplicity. Of the last and crowning work of nature, woman, the form is grace; the visage is beauty; the eye sparkles with intelligence, and smiles with soft and winning graces; the tongue is clothed with persuasion and eloquence. But what are these? A body without a soul; a combination of soft and harmonious names without a meaning; a multitude of rich inestimable gifts, heaped together in rude and inartificial confusion without the powers of enchantment and attraction. What is it that can animate the mass, that can give force and value to the whole, and reduce the shapeless chaos into form? It is simplicity, unaffected simplicity. Without thee, child of nature, daughter of the plains, beauty were no more. With thee she dwells, and in thy mansion can she only dwell. Then be the palm reserved for thee, and given to thee alone, simplicity, unaffected simplicity!"

At these words, two supernatural figures appeared below the canopy of the throne. They had the form of childen; their figures appeared so soft and waxen, that you would imagine they might be indented by the smallest touch; upon their countenances sat the lively and unexpressive smile, the sports, and the graces; and their shoulders were furnished with wings of the softest plumage, variegated with all the colours of the bow of heaven. In their hands they bore a coronet, at once rich with jewels, and light and inconsiderable in its weight. The circle was of gold, and studded with diamonds. With the diamonds were intermingled every precious gem, the topaz, the jasper, the emerald, the chrysolite, and the sapphire. The head was of Persian silk, and dyed with Tyrian purple. This coronet they placed upon the head of Imogen, and then descending to the footstool of the throne, bowed upon her feet. The song immediately recommenced.

"Imogen is under the guardianship of simplicity, her favourite pupil. Pollute not the ear of Imogen with the praises of beauty. What though her eye be full of amiableness and eloquence; what though her cheeks rival the peach, and her lips the coral; what though her bosom be soft as wax and fairer than the face of honour; what though her tresses are brighter than the shooting star? These are the bounties of nature; these are the gifts of heaven, in which she claims no merit; these are not the praises of Imogen. But this is her praise, that the graces dwell upon her lips; that her words are attired with the garb of sense and fancy; and that all her conduct is governed by the largest prudence and the nicest discretion. Heard you the sound of merriment and applause? They were the gay and unlaboured sallies of the wit of Imogen that called them forth. Saw you the look of wonder and astonishment, and the gaze of involuntary approbation and reverence? They were excited by the modesty, the circumspection, and the virtue of Imogen. And yet Imogen is artless, unaffected and innocent; her wit is unconscious of itself, and her virtue the unstudied dictate of nature. Imogen is under the guardianship of simplicity, her favourite pupil. Be hers then the crown that simplicity alone can deserve. Simplicity descends not in person to the surface of the earth; her abode is among the Gods. But Imogen is her representative, her perfect resemblance. Should simplicity descend upon the earth, she would not know herself; she would be astonished to behold another divinity, equally beautiful, equally excellent. The divinity is Imogen. Be hers then the crown, that simplicity alone can deserve."

This was a trying moment to the lovely and generous Imogen. Praise is congenial to every human sense; the voice of praise is ever grateful to the ear of virtue. The glory of the shepherd indeed lies within a narrow compass. But let immortality be named, and the heart of man is naturally attracted: it is impossible that the good and generous bosom should not long for such a prize. Nor was this all. Imogen, though loved and honoured by the borderers of Towey, had been little used to studied commendation and laboured applause. Pastoral simplicity does not deal in these; and though it seek to oblige, its endeavours are unostentatious and silent. Beside, her reverence for song was radical and deep. It had been instilled into her from her earliest infancy; from earliest infancy she had considered poetry as the vehicle of divine and eternal truth. How strange and tremendous an advantage must he gain over the ear of simplicity, who can present his fascinations under the garb of all that is sacred and all that is honourable?

The song had begun with celebrating a theme, that must for ever be congenial to every female breast. The heart of the shepherdess had instinctively vibrated to the praises of simplicity. Even the commendations bestowed upon herself were not improper, or indiscriminate; they had distinguished between the inanity of personal charms, and the value of prudence, the beauty of innocence and the merit of virtue. Even the honours she had received were attributed to these, and not to the other. Were they not therefore such as virtue would aspire to, and discretion accept?

Alas, Imogen, be not deceived with airy shadows! The reasoning may be plausible, but it is no better than sophistry. Thou must be taught, fair and unsuspecting virgin, under a beautiful outside to apprehend deceit; and to guard against the thorn which closely environs the flower. Thou must learn, loveliest of thy sex, to dread the poison of flattery. It is more venemous than the adder, it is more destructive than hebenon or madragora. It annihilates every respectable quality in the very act of extolling it; it undermines all that adorns and elevates the human character. Even now that thou listenest to it, and drinkest in, without apprehension, its opiate sounds, thou art too near to the sacrifice of those very excellencies it pretends to admire. For the head of Imogen was made giddy by the applauses she heard; drunk with admiration, she was no longer conscious of the things around her, or of herself; she sunk vanquished and supine, and was supported by one of the attendants.

At this moment Roderic came forth from an adjoining apartment, and caught in his arms the vanquished beauty. In the mean time the attendants, the musicians, and the supernatural beings disappeared, and she was left alone with her betrayer.

Roderic surveyed his victim with an eye of avidity and triumph. His eager curiosity wandered over her hoard of charms; and his brutal passion was soothed with the contemplation of her disorder. Already in imagination, he had possessed himself of a decisive advantage over so apparent a weakness; and his breast was steeled against the emotions of pity.

Imogen cast around her a languid and passive regard, and was in a moment roused from her supineness by the sight of Roderic. Her subtle adversary did not however allow her time for complete recollection, before he discovered an apparent revolution in his sentiments and language. He had heard, he said, the supernatural and celestial chorus, and been caught in the extremest degree by the praises of innocence and the trimph of virtue. He now felt the vanity and folly of those pursuits in which he had been so deeply immersed, and was determined to abjure the littleness of pride, and the emptiness of sensual gratification. He did not now address his destined prize with the commendations of beauty. He bestowed upon her with profusion the epithets of discretion, integrity, and heroism; and poured into her ear the insidious flattery, that was most soothing to her temper. Full, as he pretended, of the infant purposes of virtue, he besought his captive in the most importunate manner, to remain with him for a time, to confirm his wavering rectitude, to instruct him in duty, and thus to gain one human being to the standard of integrity, and to render so extensive possessions subservient to the happiness of mankind. All this he expressed with that ardour, which is congenial to the simplicity of truth; and with that enthusiasm, which in all instances accompanies recent conviction.

Imogen was totally uninured to the contemplation of hypocrisy, and immediately yielded the most unreserved credit to these professions. Her joy was extreme at the change in the dispositions of Roderic, and her admiration of the irresistible charms of rectitude pious and profound. The praises bestowed upon her seemed distinguishing and sincere, and she drank them in with the most visible complacency. She expressed however an ingenuous diffidence of her capacity for the task of an instructor, and she intreated at any rate to be permitted to withdraw for a short time to dry up the tears of her disconsolate parents.

These difficulties were too obvious to create any embarrassment to so consummate a deceiver. He described the danger of that vicious mistrust of our powers, that is the enemy of all generous and heroic action. He reminded his captive how recent were his purposes, and how many unforeseen incidents might be crowded into so eventful a moment. There were goblins, he said, ever ready to seduce the wanderer from his wished return; and he had been too much their prey not to have every thing to dread from the subtlety of their machinations. On the other hand, no character was suspended on the longer or shorter duration of the uneasiness of the parents of Imogen; and the joyful surprise they would ere long experience, might abundantly compensate for any temporary anxiety and solicitude. He told her of the worship and reverence that were due to the immortal Gods. Could she imagine that the scene that had just passed was produced for the mere honour and gratification of a virtuous character, than for the instruction of the ignorant, and the restoration of the wandering? Shall she be thus honoured, and shall this be her gratitude?

Though the web of the sophistry woven by her betrayer might seem inextricable, though Imogen had no sentiments more predominant than the love of virtue, and the fear of the Gods, yet her heart involuntarily resisted his persuasions, and she felt the yearnings of affection still active in her bosom towards those, to whom she owed her existence.

"And cannot you," cried the lovely maiden, "attend me in the short absense I demand? That would prevent every danger, and supersede every objection." "Ah, shepherdess," replied the magician, "this reluctance, these studied expedients imply diffidence and disobedience. But diffidence is much unworthy of the heart of Imogen. Your life has been marked with one tenour of piety. Do not then begin to disobey. Do not sully the unspotted whiteness of your character."

"This," rejoined Imogen, "is too much. This is mere savageness of virtue. Why in the act of persuading me do you bestow upon me those laboured commendations, which the very persuasions you employ are intended to prove that I little deserve? Is it necessary, Roderic, that your manners should be so strange and unaccountable, as to supply food for eternal jealousy and suspicion? And what must be that conduct, that inspires jealousy into a heart unguarded as mine? I talk of suspicion, but I scarcely know the meaning of the term. And yet there is in your carriage something precise, plausible and composed, that I have seldom observed in any other man. Oh, shepherd! you know not what you do, when you awake all these ideas in a maiden's breast, when you thus confound things that heaven and earth put asunder."

"Ungenerous Imogen," replied the magician, "wherefore this? Do I claim any thing more of you than rectitude demands, and your own bosom will another day approve? Am I not your better genius to guard you against the errors that might be prompted by too tender a heart? Beside, does the conduct of beings of a higher order depend upon my nod? Can I control the spheres, and call down celestial essences from their bright abodes? And will they be rendered subservient to the purposes of treachery and guilt?"

"Roderic here break we off our conference. Sure I am that your conduct is not dictated by a regard for my ease or my welfare. How unworthy then, as well as how unjust is the pretence? With respect to the supernatural scenes I have beheld, the question is more difficult. Of such I have heard from the mouth of the conse-crated priests, but never till this day did I see them. At present however my mind is too much distracted, to be able to decide. I have already gone far enough; as far as my heart will permit me. I must now retire.'

"One thing however I will add. From the resolutions you at first professed, and the impressions you appeared to feel, I had conceived the most sanguine hopes, and the sincerest pleasure. These are all now vanished. I cannot account for this. But your conduct is now as mysterious to my comprehension, as it was before disgusting to my judgment. I am bewildered in a maze of uncertainty. I am lost in unwelcome obscurity. May your resolutions and designs be better than my hopes! But ah, Roderic, for how much have you to answer, how deep must be your guilt, if all this be mummery, dissimulation, and hypocrisy!"

The magician perceived that it was in vain to urge the stratagem any further, and he retired from the presence of the shepherdess in silence. If he had been able to distract her ingenuous mind between contending duties, he had not however succeeded in his principal object, that of undermining her virtue, and lessening her attachment to her parents and her lover. If Imogen were perplexed and con-founded, Roderic was scarcely more happy. He looked back upon the scene with mortification and astonishment. It was difficult for him to determine where it had digressed from the auspicious appearances it had at first exhibited, and yet he found himself in the conclusion of it wide, very wide indeed, of the success of which he had aimed.

"To what purpose," exclaimed he, with a voice of anguish and rage, "have I in-herited the most inexhaustible riches? To what purpose is the command which I boast over the goblins of the abyss, if one weak, simple, and uninstructed woman shall thus defy my arts? I call the hills my own. I mount upon the turrets of my castle, and as far as my eye can survey, the bending corn and the grazing herds belong to me. My palace is adorned with all that can sooth the wearied frame, or gratify the luxurious desire. Couches of purple, and services of gold, the most exquisite viands, and the blandishments of enticing beauty, charms of which the ruggedness of pastoral life has not so much as the idea, all these are circled within my walls. Beyond all this, I command myriads of spirits, invisible, and reputedly omnipotent. If I but stamp my foot, if I but wave this wand, they fly swifter than the wings of thought to my presence. One look of favour inspires them with tranquility and exultation; one frown of displeasure terrifies them into despair. I dispatch them far as the corners of the moon. At my bidding they engage in the most toilsome enterprises, and undertake the labour of revolving years. Oh impotence of power! oh mockery of state! what end can ye now serve but to teach me to be miserable? Power, the hands of which are chained and fettered in links of iron; state, which is bestowed only like a paper crown to adorn the brows of a baby, are the most cruel aggravations of disappointment, the most fearful insults upon the weak. But shall I always obey the imperious mandate?"

"Yes, Roderic, thou shalt obey," exclaimed the inimical goblin, who at this moment burst through a condensed cloud, that had arisen unperceived in one corner of the apartment, and appeared before him. "In vain dost thou struggle with the links of destiny. In vain dost thou exert thyself to escape from the fillets that on every side surround thee. The greater and the more obstinate are thy efforts, the more closely art thou bound, and the more inextricably engaged. This is the situation in which I wished to see thee. Every pang it wrings from thy heart, every exclamation it forces from thy tongue, is solace to my thoughts, and music to my ears. And wert thou vain and weak enough to imagine, that riches would purchase thee every pleasure, that riches would furnish an inexhaustible source of enjoyment? Of all mortal possessions they are the most useless, mischievous, and baleful. The Gods, when the Gods are willing to perfect a character of depravity, in order to make vice consummately detestable, or to administer an exemplary punishment to distinguished wickedness, bestow upon that man, as the last of curses, and the most refined of tortures, extensive possessions and unbounded riches. Indulge to the mistaken pride which these inspire, and wrap thyself up in the littleness of thy heart. — But no, rise above them. Suffer thy desires to wander into a larger and more dangerous field. Run with open eyes into the mouth of that destruction that gapes to devour thee! Why shouldst thou attend to the voice of destiny, to the immutable laws of the Gods, and the curse that is suspended over thee? Be a man. Bravely defy all that is most venerable, and all that is most unchangeable. Oh how I long for thy ruin! How my heart pants for the illustrious hour in which thy *palaces shall be crumbled down to the dust of the balance, thy riches scattered, and thyself become an unpitied, necessitous, miserable vagabond!* In the mean time, remember, that riches like thine are not bestowed with u[n]reserving hand, that commerce is not permitted with the shadows of darkness, without some trifling fall to ill amid this immensity of uniform happiness. For this end I am commissioned from time to time to appear before thee in the midst of thy triumph, and to mingle with thy exultations the boding voice of prophetic woe."

Roderic did not listen to these bitter sarcasms without exhibiting every mark of fury and impatience. At length he commanded the spectre to depart, with a voice so fierce and stern as to terrify him into submission. For though the authority of the magician was not formidable enough to make him desist from persecuting him, yet the penalties he had frequently been able to inflict, inspired the goblin in spite of himself, with the fear of so potent an adversary. Still choked however with agony and resentment, Roderic waved his wand, and summoned his favourite instrument and the prime minister of his pleasures, the goblin Medoro, to his presence. The moment he appeared the magician was relieved from that violent gust of passion, which had held him motionless, a statue of horror, and throwing himself upon his couch, he burst into a flood of tears.

Medoro was the goblin that had appeared to Edwin in his return from the feast of the bards, and had brewed the fatal storm that had preceded the rape of Imogen. The figure of the spectre was uncouth, and his countenance was full of savage and shapeless deformity. Nor did his appearance bely his character. To all other beings, whether of the terrestrial or the invisible world, his temper was hard, impracticable and remorseless. To Rodogune alone, a similitude of minds, and a congenial ferocity of heart had attached him; and the attachment had descended to her son; though not equally destitute of every agreeable and every plausible quality. He therefore beheld the affliction of Roderic with sympathy and compassion.

"Wherefore," cried Medoro, modulating a voice, that nature had made up of dissonance and horror, into the most gentle and soothing accent of which it was capable, and hanging over his couch, "wherefore this sorrow? What is it that has seemed to mar a happiness so enviable? Art thou not possessed" — "Talk not to me of possessions," exclaimed Roderic, with a tone of frenzy, and starting from his posture, "I give them to the winds. I banish them from my thoughts for ever. Oh that the earth would open and swallow them up! Oh that unburdened from them all, I were free as the children of the vallies, and careless as the shepherd that carols to the rising day. I had not then been thus entangled in misfortune, thus every way closed in to remediless despair. I had not then been a monument of impotence and misery for the world to gaze at. Ye are all combined against me! Under a specious, smiling countenance you all conceal a heart of gall. But your hypocrisy and your mummery shall serve you to little purpose. Point me, this instant point me, to a path for the gratification of my wishes, or dearly shall you rue the shallowness of your invention and the treachery of your professions."

Medoro was astonished at the vehemence of the passion of Roderic, unusual even in a youth who had never been refused demands the most unreasonable, and who had been inured to see all the powers of nature bend to his will. "Is this," cried he, "a return for services so unwearied and sincere as mine? Foolish and ungrateful youth! But I will point you to a remedy. Had you not been blinded with fury and impatience, you would have seen that your situation was not yet irremediable, by means the most obviously in your power. Did I not at your birth bestow upon you a ring, that communicates to the wearer the power of assuming what form he please? I gave it, in order to elude the curse of the malignant goblin, to subdue the most obdurate female, and to evade the most subtle adversary. The uses in which thou hast hitherto employed it have been idle and capricious, gov-

erned by whim, and dictated by the sallies of a sportive fancy. It is now first that
an opportunity is offered to turn it to those purposes for which it was more immediately destined. Dost thou not now address an obdurate maid? Is she not full of
constancy and attachment for another? What avails it then to a heart, simple and
unvitiated as hers, to offer the bribe of riches, and to lavish the incense of flattery and adulation. Attack her in her love. Appear to her in the form of him to whom
she is most ardently attached. If Imogen is vulnerable, this is the quarter from
which she must be approached. Thus far Roderic thou mayest try thy power; but
if by this avenue thou canst not surprise her heart and overpower her virtue, be
then wise. Recollect thy courage, strengthen thy resolution, and shake off for ever
a capricious inclination, which interrupts the tenour of a life that might otherwise
wear the uniform colour of happiness."

The information of a new measure for the furthering his darling pursuit, was a
communication of the most reviving kind to the heart of Roderic. The gloom and
petulance that had collected upon his countenance were dissipated in a moment.
His cheek caught anew the flush of expectation; his eye sparkled anew with the
insolence of victory. His gratitude to the propitious Medoro was now as immod-
erate as his displeasure had lately been unreasonable. He walked along the apartments with the stride of exultation and triumph. He forgot the pathetic exclama-
tions he had lately uttered upon the impotence of power, and he was full of congratulation in the possession of that which he had treated with contempt. The
moral lessons which it was his destiny to have from time to time poured into an
unwilling ear were erased for ever. He exclaimed upon his own stupidity and
want of invention, and he remembered not that vehemence of passion, which had
distracted his understanding, and drawn a cloud over all his ideas. It was not
instantly that he could assume a sufficient degree of collectedness and composure
to put into execution the scheme with which he was so highly delighted. Presently
however the ebriety of unexpected hope dissipated, and he prepared for that
scene which was to be regarded as the summit of his power, and the irrevocable
crisis of his fate.

BOOK the FIFTH

THE GARDEN OF RODOGUNE DESCRIBED.—THE HOPES
AND DANGER OF IMOGEN.—HER INCONSOLABLE DISTRESS.

IMOGEN, immediately after the interview that had so deeply perplexed her,
returning to her apartment, had shut herself up in solitude. Her reflections
were gloomy and unpleasing; the new obscurity that hung about them had not
contributed to lighten their pressure. But though she was melancholy, her melancholy was of a different hue from that of her ravisher. If virtue can ever be deprived of those glorious distinctions that exclusively belong to her, it must be
when she is precluded from the illuminations of duty, and is no longer able to
discern the path in which she ought to tread. But even here, where distinction
seems most annihilated, it yet remains. The cruel sensations of Imogen were not
aggravated by despair, but heightened by hope. Through them all she was sus-
tained by the consciousness of her rectitude. The chearfulness of innocence supported her under every calamity.

She had not long remained alone before she was summoned to partake of that
plainer repast, which in the œconomy of Roderic usually occupied the middle of
the day, and preceded the sumptuous and splendid entertainment of the evening,
by which the soul was instigated to prolong the indulgence of the table, and to
throw the reins upon the neck of enjoyment. But Imogen, whose thoughts were
dark, and whose mind brooded over a thousand sad ideas, was desirous of that
solitude, which in the simplicity of pastoral life is ever at hand. She could not
away with the freedom of society, and the levity of mirth. It was painful to her to
have any witnesses of her new sensations, and she wished to remove herself for
ever from the inspection of the officious and the inquisitive. In compliance with
her humour a few viands were served to her in her own apartment. She was induced by the entreaties of her attendant, to call up a momentary smile upon her
countenance, and to endeavour to partake of the refreshment that was offered her.
But the effort was vain. It was the sunshine of an April day; her repast in spite of
her was bedewed with tears, and she ate the bread of sorrow.

As soon as it was concluded, she was invited to a short excursion in the garden
of the mansion. Unused to refusal, the natural mildness of her temper inclined to
comply. She saw the necessity of not yielding herself up to passive and unresisting
melancholy. The natural serenity of innocence did not yet permit her to be insensible to the attractions of enjoyment; and the transient view she had had of the
garden, as she passed to the terrace, led her to expect from it, something that might
sooth her pensive thoughts, and something that might divert her affliction.

The garden of Rodogune was an inclosure in a bottom glade, at the entrance of
which, though nigh to the castle, and upon a lower ground, you wholly lost sight
of the mansion, and every external object. But though these were excluded, the
sorceress by her art had also excluded the appearance of limits and boundaries.
The scene was not terminated by walls and espaliers, but by the entrance on

either side of a wild, meandring wood. The side by which you were introduced was protected by trees of the thickest foliage; and the gate was masqued with a clump of hazels and alders, which permitted only two narrow passages on either side. The eye was shut in, but the imagination was permitted to range in perfect freedom. Nor was this seeming confinement calculated to disgust; on the contrary you willingly believed that every charm and every grace was shut up in the circle, and you trembled lest the smallest outlet should take off from the richness of the scene. In entering you were struck with a sensation of coolness, that impervious shades, a bright and animated verdure, flowers scattered here and there in agreeable disorder, the prattling of the stream, and the song of a thousand birds, impressed as strongly upon the imagination, as the senses. But this did not appear the result of art. Every thing had the face of uncultivated luxuriance, and impenetrable solitude. You could not believe that you were not the first mortal that had ever found his way into the enchanting desert.

The scene however had been solely produced by the skill of Rodogune. Erewhile the grass had appeared dry and parched; a few solitary and leafless trees had been scattered up and down; there was no gaiety of colours to relieve the eye; and not one drop of water to give freshness to the prospect. But with the operations of magic Rodogune had delighted to supersede the parsimony of nature. She caused the tree and the shrub to spring forth in the richest abundance; the sturdiness of whose trunks, or the deepness of their verdure, cheated the eye with the semblance of the ripening hand of time. She sprinkled the turf, short, fine, and vivid, with flowers both native and exotic. She called forth a thousand fountains to enrich the scene. Sometimes they crept beneath the turf in almost imperceptible threads; sometimes they ran beside the alleys, or crossed them in sportive wantonness; and sometimes you might see them in broader and more limpid currents rolling over a smooth and spotted bed. Now they rose from the soil in foamy violence, and fell upon the chalk and pebbly ground beneath; and anon they formed themselves into the deeper bason [sic], whose calm and even surface reflected back the reeds and shrubs that were planted round. There was nothing strait and nothing level; the rule and the line had never entered the delicious spot; the irregularities of the soil, and the fantastic, gradual windings of the alleys, were calculated to give length to the passage, and immensity to the scene.

From time to time you encountered tufts of trees closely planted, and that cast as brown a shade as the thickest forest. These were partly composed of wood of the most pliant texture, the extremities of whose branches, bending to the earth, took root a second time in her bosom. Elsewhere the rasberry [sic], the rose, the lilac, and a thousand flowering shrubs, appeared in thickets without either regularity or symmetry, and contributed at once to adorn, and to give an air of rudeness and wildness to the prospect. Round the body of the trees, planted some at their root, and some upon the different parts of the trunk, crept the withy, the snakeweed, the ivy, and the hop, and intermingled with them the jessamine and the honeysuckle, in the most unbounded profusion. Their tendrils hung from the branches, and waved to the wind; and suggested to you the appearance of garlands scattered from tree to tree by the nymphs of the grove. All was inexpressible luxuriance, and a thousand different shades of verdure were placed, one upon another, in regular confusion, and attractive disorder. An exuberance of this sort was calculated in a vulgar scene to have checked the fertility of the plants, and to have given a sickly and withered appearance to their productions; but it was not so in the garden of Rodogune. There the cherry and the grape, the downy peach and the purple plum were half discovered amid the foliage of the hop, and the clusters of the woodbine. Beneath the delicious shade you wandered over beds of moss, undeformed with barren sands and intrusive weeds, and smooth as the level face of ocean when all the winds of heaven sleep.

Nor was this all. Inanimate and vegetable nature (and the observation had not escaped the penetration of Rodogune) adorn and arrange it as you will, infallibly suggests an idea of solitude, that communicates sadness to the mind. Accordingly your path was here beguiled with the warbling of a thousand birds, the full-toned blackbird, the mellow thrush, and the pensive nightingale. The sorceress had invited them to her retreat, by innumerable assiduities and innumerable conveniences of food and residence, and had suffered no rude intrusion to disturb the sacredness of their haunts. Unused to molestation in all their pursuits, they now showed no terror of human approach, but flew, and hopped, and sung, and played among the branches and along the ground, in thoughtless security and wanton defiance.

For a few moments Imogen was immersed in the contemplation of the beauties of the place, and its delightful coolness and mingled fragrance were balm and softness to her wounded soul. The domestic who accompanied her, perceived her propensity to reflection and fell back to a small distance. The shepherdess, as soon as she found herself disengaged and alone, revolved with the utmost displeasure her present situation. "How happy," cried she, "are the virgins of the vale! To them every hour is winged with tranquility and pleasure. They laugh at sorrow; they trill the wild, unfettered lay, or wander, chearful and happy, with the faithful swain beneath the woodland shade. They fear no coming mischief; they know not the very meaning of an enemy. Innocent themselves, they apprehend not guilt and treachery in those around them. Nor have they reason. Simplicity and frankness are the unvaried character of the natives of the plain. Liberty, immortal, unvalued liberty, is the daughter of the mountains. We suspected not that deceit, insidiousness, and slavery were to be found beneath the sun. Ah, why was I selected from the rest to learn the fatal lesson! Unwished, unfortunate distinction! Was I, who am simple and undisguised as the light of day, who know not how to conceal one sentiment of my heart, or arm myself with the shield of vigilance and incredulity, was I fitted by nature for a scene like this? In the mean time have not the Gods encouraged me by the most splendid appearance, and the most animating praises? I would not impeach their venerable counsels. But was this a time for applauses so seducing? How greatly have they perplexed, and how deeply distressed me! In what manner, alas! are they to be obeyed, and what am I to think of the professions of my ravisher? But, no; I dare not permit my purpose to be thus suspended. My danger here is too imminent. The deliverance of my own honour and the felicity of my parents are motives too sacred, not to annihilate every ambiguity and every doubt. Oh, that I could escape at once! Oh, that like the tender bird, that hops before me in my path, I could flit away along the trackless air! Why should the little birds that carol among the trees be the only beings in the domains of Roderic, that know the sweets of liberty? But it will not be. Still, still I am under the eye and guardianship of heaven. Wise are the ways of heaven, and I submit myself with reverence. Only do ye, propitious Gods, support, sustain, deliver me! Never was frail and trembling mortal less prepared to encounter with machination, and to brave unheard of dangers. How fearful are those I have already encountered; and how much have I to apprehend from what may yet remain! But if I am weak, the omnipotent support to which I look is strong. I will not give way to impious despondence. It has delivered, and it may yet deliver me."

By such virtuous and ingenuous reflections the shepherdess endeavoured to solace her distress, and to fortify her courage. Now by revolving her dangers she sought to prepare for their encounter; and now she dismissed the recollection as too depressing and too melancholy. The confinedness of the prospect, though rich infinitely beyond any thing she had yet seen, and though not naturally calculated to fatigue and disgust, was destructive of all its beauty in the eyes of Imogen. It presented to her too just an image of the thraldom, which was the subject of all her complaints. She desired to fling her eye through a wider prospect; and though unable even from the loftiest ground to discover the happy valley, she coveted the slender gratification of beholding the utmost boundaries of the magic circle, and extending her view as near as possible to her beloved home. She therefore advanced farther in the garden, and presently arrived at a clear and open brow, where a beautiful alcove was erected to catch the point of view, from which the surrounding objects appeared in the greatest variety, and with the happiest effect. She entered; and the domestic that attended her remained in a distant part of the garden.

Scarcely had Imogen seated herself, before she discovered, by a casual glance over the prospect, and at some distance, a youth, who seemed to advance with hasty steps towards the castle. At first she was tempted to turn away her eye with carelessness and inattention. There was however something in his figure, that led her, by a kind of fascination for which she could not account, to cast upon him a second glance and a third. He drew nearer. He leaped with an active bound over the fence that separated him from the garden. It was the form of Edwin. His hair hung carelessly about his shoulders. His shepherd's pipe was slung in his belt. His clear and manly cheeks glowed with the warmth of the day, and the anxiety of love. He entered the alcove.

Had a ghost risen before Imogen, surrounded with all the horrors of the abyss, she could not have been struck with greater astonishment. As he advanced, she gazed in silence. She could not utter a word. Her very breath seemed suppressed. At length he entered, and for a moment she had voice enough to utter her surprise. "Gracious powers!" exclaimed she — "is it possible? — what is it that I see? — Edwin, beloved Edwin!" — and she sunk breathless upon her seat. The fictitious shepherd approached her, folded her in his arms, and with repeated, burning kisses, which he had never before ventured to ravish from his disdainful captive, restored her to life and perception. The confusion of Imogen did not allow her to animadvert upon his freedoms. She had the utmost confidence in the person whose form he wore, and the guileless simplicity of pastoral life is accustomed to permit many undesigning liberties, and is slow to take the alarm, or to suspect a sinister purpose.

Roderic, anxious and timid respecting the success of his adventure, was backward to enter into conversation. Imogen, on the other hand, charmed with so unexpected an appearance, and presaging from it the most auspicious consequences, full of her situation and sufferings, and having a thousand things that pressed at once to be told, was eager and impatient to communicate them to her faithful shepherd. She was also desirous of learning by what undiscoverable means, by what happy fortune, he had been conducted to this impervious retreat, and at so critical a juncture. "Edwin, — my gallant Edwin, — how came you hither? — Sure it was some propitious power, — some unseen angel, — that conducted you. — Oh, my friend, — I have been miserable, — perplexed — tortured — but it is now no more — I will not think of it — Thanks to the immortal Gods, I have no occasion — no room — but for gratitude. — Edwin — what have you done — and how did you escape the tempest? — Was it not a fearful storm? — But I ask you a thousand questions — and you do not answer me. — You seem abashed — uncertain — what is the meaning of this? — Did you not come to succour my distress? — Was it not pity for your poor — forlorn — desolate Imogen — that directed your steps?"

"Yes, loveliest of thy sex," replied her betrayer. "I flew upon the wings of love. I was brought along by a celestial, impulsive guidance, which I followed I knew not why. Oh how gracious the condescension, how happy the obedience, how grateful the interview! Yes, Imogen, I was in despair. I was terrified at the concurring prodigies by which we were separated, and I feared never, never to behold that beauteous form again. Come then and let me clasp thee to my bosom. Oh, thou art sweeter than the incense-breathing rose, and brighter than the lily of the vale!"

For a moment, the affectionate and unsuspicious shepherdess received his caresses with complacence and pleasure. Suddenly however she recollected herself; instinctively and without reflection she repulsed the undue warmth of his attentions. "This," cried she, "is no time for fond indulgence, and careless dalliance — Fate is on the wing. — Our situation is arduous — and we are in the midst of enemies. — Every thing that surrounds us is full of danger — all is deceit and treachery — appearances are insidious — all is frightful suspense and headlong precipice. — The plotter of my ruin is as potent as he is — Ah! every hour is big with calamity and destruction — every moment that we stay here is in the last degree hazardous and decisive. — My keepers may be alarmed — Those eyes that never close may be summoned to attention — we may be hemmed in — prevented — Oh, Edwin, how fearful is this place — and how unhoped — how joyful to me — must be an escape. — I thought this hated seat had been impervious and impassable — Hark! — Did you not hear the sound of feet? — No — every thing is still — Let us go this way — Say, by what path did you come — Let us hasten our flight — let us make no delay — not look behind."

"Yes, Imogen," replied Roderic, detaining her, "we will escape — But this, my lovely maiden, is not the time — I am not yet prepared — We may remain here in security — already the shades of evening begin to draw. Every thing is now busy and active. We cannot pass from hence without observation. In the silence of the night the attempt will be more practicable. And you, Imogen, are a heroine. The Gods will watch over us. Silence and darkness have nothing in them at which innocence should be terrified. Till then let us reconcile ourselves to our situation. Let us endeavour, by secrecy and stilness, not to attract to us the attention of the enemies with which we are surrounded. Let us banish from them curiosity and suspicion. And let us trust in the Gods, propitious to rectitude, that they will look down with favour upon a design prompted by virtue and urged by oppression."

"Alas, Edwin," replied the shepherdess "it is with regret that I consent to remain one moment longer in this fatal spot. But I will submit to your direction, I will confide in your prudence; I will trust in your fidelity, and your zeal, for the deliverance I so ardently desire. Here however we cannot long remain undiscovered. — My absence will be suspicious. — I will return once again to the hated mansion. — You, my swain, must conceal yourself in the mazes of this friendly wilderness. It shall not be long ere I come to you again. — With motives like mine to inspire ingenuity, I shall easily find a way to elude the strictest guard, and escape from the closest thraldom. — Say, my Edwin! — this stratagem shall suffice, — and you shall lead me in safety under the friendly cover of the night to liberty and innocence!"

"Yes," exclaimed Roderic, suddenly recollecting himself, "you may be assured that by me nothing shall be omitted, that can further your escape from this detested prison. The perils I have already incurred may well convince you of this. It has been through the most fearful dangers, ready every moment to be overwhelmed with omnipotent mischief, that I have reached you. I have approached by the most devious and undiscovered paths. Though the greatest hazards are to be encountered in the cause of innocence and honour, the conduct we should pursue is therefore ambiguous, and our success involved in uncertainty and darkness. Oh Imogen, I may now behold thee for the last time. The moment we sally from this retreat, I may be discovered by that enemy from whom we have so much to fear. I may be confined to all the wantonness of inventive torture, and that beauteous form, and the smiles of that bewitching countenance may be torn from these longing eys for ever. But here, my shepherdess, we are safe. We may here secure ourselves from sudden intrusion, and a thousand means of concealment are here in our power. This Imogen is the moment of our ascendancy, this little period is all our own. In a short time the precious hours will be elapsed, the invaluable instants will be run out. Oh, my love, fairest, most angelic of thy sex, while they are yet ours, let us improve them." — He ceased; and his countenance glistened with the anticipations of enjoyment, and his eyes emitted the sparkles of lust.

But the imagination of Imogen was not sullied with the impressions of indecency, and the baseness of looser desires. She understood not the innuendos of

Roderic, and she remarked not with an eager and inquisitive eye the distraction of his visage. She replied therefore only to the more obvious tendency of what he said. "And is this, Edwin, all the consolation you bring me? Ah how poor, how heartless, and how cold! If we accomplish not that flight upon which my hopes and wishes are suspended, what utility and what pleasure can we derive from this interview? It will then only be a bitter aggravation of all my trials, and all my miseries. If a prospect so unexpected and desirable terminate in no advantage, for what purpose was it opened before me? It will but render my sensations more poignant, and give a new refinement to the exquisiteness of despair.

"But no, my Edwin, let us not give way to despondence. The Gods, my generous swain, the same Gods that give luxuriance and felicity to the plain, and that have guided you through every hazard to this impervious spot, will assuredly deliver us. Remember the lessons of the heaven-taught Druids. There is an innate dignity and omnipotence in virtue. She may be surrounded with variety of woes, but none of them shall approach her. The darts of calamity may assail her on every side, but she is invulnerable to them all. Before her majesty, the fierceness of all the tenants of the wood is disarmed, and the more untamed brutality of savage man is awed into mute obedience. She may not indeed put on the insolence of pride, and the fool-hardiness of presumption. But wherever her duty calls, she may proceed fearless and unhurt. She may be attacked, but she cannot be wounded: she may be surprised, but she cannot be enslaved: she may be obscured for a moment, but it shall only be to burst forth again more illustrious than ever.

"But you, Edwin, are much better acquainted with these things, and more able to instruct than I. They were ever the favourite subject of your attention. I have seen you with rooted eye fixed for hours in listening admiration of the sublime dictates of the hoary Llewelyn. — It is little to learn, to understand, and to admire. A barren and ineffectual enthusiasm for the speculations of truth, was never respectable and was never venerable. Now, my swain, is the moment in which these sacred lessons are to be called into action, and in which, beyond all others, reputation is to be asserted and character fixed. Leave not then to me the business of inciting and animating you. Be you my leader and protector."

"Alas, my charming mistress," replied her admirer, "I would to God it were in my power to inspire you with hope and fill you with courage. I confess that while peril was at a distance, and I sat secure in the tranquil vale, I received without distinction the doctrines of the Druids, and bowed assent to their sacred lessons. But practice, my Imogen, and the scenes of danger differ beyond conception from the ideas we form of them in the calmness of repose. Something must be allowed to the unruffled solitude of these sacred men, and something to the sublime of poetry. Surely it is no part of comprehensive prudence to banish the idea of those hazards that must be encountered, and to refuse to survey the snares and the difficulties with which our path is surrounded. Remember, my fair one, the malignant suspiciousness of your jailer, and the comfortless darkness of the night." —

"Oh Edwin, and is this the strain in which you were wont to talk? Why are you thus altered, and what means this inauspicious quick-sightedness and alarm? We should indeed survey and prepare for danger, but we should never suffer it to overwhelm us. The cause of integrity should never be despaired of. What avails the suspicions of my keeper? The ever wakeful eye of heaven can make them slumber. Why should we reck the gloom and loneliness of the night? Virtue is the ever-burning lamp of the sacred groves. No darkness can cast a shadow on her beams. Though the sun and moon were hurled below the bosom of the circling ocean, virtue could see to perform her purposes, and execute her great designs. Alas, my swain, my voice is weak, and broken, and powerless. But willingly would I breathe a soul to animate your timidity. Oh Edwin," and she folded him in her alabaster arms to her heaving, anxious bosom, "let me not exhort you in vain! It is but for a little while, it is but for one short effort, and if the powers above smile propitious on our purpose, we are happy for ever! Think how great and beautiful is our adventure. Comfortless and desponding as I am now, ready to sink without life and animation at your feet, I may be in a few hours happier than ever. — Oh Edwin, lead on! — Can you hesitate? — Would it were in my power to reward the virtue I would excite as it deserves to be rewarded. But the Gods will reward you, Edwin." —

As she uttered these words, her action was unspeakably graceful, her countenance was full of persuasion, and her voice was soft, and eloquent, and fascinating. Roderic gazed upon her with insatiate curiosity, and drank her accents with a greedy ear. For a moment, charmed with the loftiness of her discourse and the heroism of her soul, he was half persuaded to relent, and abjure his diabolical purpose. It was only by summoning up all the fierceness of his temper, all the impatience of his passions, and all the mistaken haughtiness and inflexibility of his purpose, that he could resist the artless enchantment. During the internal struggle, his countenance by no means answered to the simplicity of pastoral sentiments. It was now fierce, and now unprotected and despairing. Anon it was pale with envy, and anon it was flushed with the triumph of brutal passion. Transitions like these could not pass unobserved. Imogen beheld them with anxiety and astonishment, but suspicion was too foreign in her breast, to be thus excited.

"Imogen," cried the traitor, "it is in your power to reward the noblest acts of heroism that human courage can perform. Who in the midst of all the exultation and applause that triumphant rectitude can inspire, could look to a nobler prize than the condescension of your smiles and the heaven of your embraces? No, too amiable shepherdess, it is not for myself I fear; witness every action of my life; witness all those dangers that I have this moment unhesitatingly encountered, that I might fly to your arms. But, oh, when your safety is brought to hazard, I feel that I am indeed a coward. Think, my fair one, of the dangers that surround us. Let us calmly revolve, before we immediately meet them. No sooner shall we set our foot beyond this threshold, than they will commence. Tyranny is ever full of apprehensions and environed with guards. Along the gallery, and through the protracted hall, centinels are placed with every setting sun. Could you escape their observations, an hundred bolts, and an hundred massive chains secure the hinges of the impious mansion. Beyond it all will be dark, and the solitude inviolate. But suppose we meet again, — by what path to cross the wide extended glade, and to reach the only avenue that can lead us safely through this horrid cincture, will then be undiscoverable. Amid the untamed forest and untrod precipices that lie beyond, all the beasts most inimical to man reside. There the hills re-echo the tremendous roarings of the boar; the serpents hiss among the thickets; and the gaunt and hungry wolf roams for prey. Oh, Imogen, how fearful is the picture! And can your tender frame, and your timid spirits support the reality?"

Imogen had now preserved the character of heroism and fortitude for a considerable time. All the energies of her soul had been exerted to encounter the trials and surmount the difficulties which she felt to be unavoidable. When the beloved form of Edwin had appeared before her, she relaxed in some degree from the caution and vigilance she had hitherto preserved. It is the very nature of joyful surprize to unbend as it were the strings of the mind, and to throw wide the doors of unguarded confidence. Before, she had felt herself alone; she saw no resource but in her own virtue, and could lean upon no pillar but her own resolution. Now she had trusted to meet with an external support; she had poured out her heart into the bosom of him in whom she confided, and she looked to him for prudence, for suggestion and courage. But, instead of support, she had found debility, and instead of assistance the resources of her own mind were dried up, and her native fortitude was overwhelmed and depressed. She turned pale at the recital of Roderic, her knees trembled, her eyes forgot their wonted lustre, and she was immersed in the supineness and imbecility of despair.

"Edwin!" — she cried, with a tone of perturbation; but her utterance failed her. Her voice was low, hoarse, and inaudible. The fictitious shepherd supported her in his arms. Her distress was a new gratification and stimulus to her betrayer. "Edwin, ah, wherefore this fearful recital? Did you come here for no other purpose than to sink me ten times deeper in despair? Alas, I had conceived far other expectations, and far other hopes fluttered in my anxious bosom, when I first beheld your well known form. I said I have been hitherto constant and determined, though unsupported and melancholy. I shall now be triumphant. I shall experience that heaven-descended favour, which ever attends the upright. Edwin, my firm, heroic Edwin, will perform what I wished, and finish what I began. And, oh, generous and amiable shepherd, is it thus that my presages are fulfilled? No, I cannot, will not bear it. If the courage of Edwin fail, I will show him what he ought to be. If you dare not lead, think whether you dare follow whither I guide. You shall see what an injured and oppressed woman can do. Feeble and tender as we are formed by nature, you shall see that we are capable of some fortitude and some exertion." As she said this she had risen, and was advancing towards the door. But recollecting herself with a sudden pang, "Alas," cried she, "whither do I go? — What am I doing? — What shall I do? — Oh, Edwin!" and, falling at his feet, she embraced his knees, "do not, do no [sic] not desert me in this sad, tremendous moment!"

"I will not, my Imogen, I will never desert you. One fate shall attend us both. And if you are called to calamity, to torture, and to death, Edwin will not be supine and inactive." "Oh, now," cried she, her eyes moistened with rapture, "I recognize my noble and gallant swain. Come then, and let us fly. If we must encounter peril and disaster, what avails it to suspend the trial for a few niggard hours? This, my friend, my guardian, — this is the time — Now the master dragon sleeps — Roderic is now unconscious and distant — and I fear him too much to apprehend any thing from a meaner adversary — Let us fly — let us escape — let our speed outstrip the rapid winds!"

During their conversation, the heavens had been covered with clouds, and the rain descended with violence. But the change had not been noticed by Imogen. "Well then, my fair one, we will depart. What though the wind whistles along the heath, and the rain patters among the elms? We will defy their fury. Let us go! But, ah, my Imogen, look there! The hinds are flying across the plain for shelter; and see! two of them approach to the clump of trees directly before us on the outside of the garden. No, shepherdess, it is in vain that we resolve, and in vain that we struggle: we cannot escape."

The mind of Imogen was now wrought up to the extremest distress. Her heart was wrung with anguish. She was ready to charge the immortals with conspiring against her, had not her piety forbad it. She saw the reality of what Roderic stated, and yet she was ready to charge him with raising eternal obstacles. She cast upon him a look of despair and agony. But she did not read in the countenance of the imaginary shepherd congenial sentiments. "Methinks," said she, with a voice full of reproachful blandishment, and inimitable sweetness, "methinks it is not with the tenderness of sympathy, that you tell me we must desist. Sure it is only the mist of tears through which I behold you, that makes me see the suppressed emotion of pleasure in your countenance. No, it is not in the heart of Edwin to harbour for a moment the sentiments of barbarity and insult — But if we cannot now escape — if the dangers to which we must submit may be diminished by delay — indeed, Edwin, something must be attempted — at least let us now fix upon a plan, and determine what to do. Let not delay relax the spirit of enterprise, or shake the firmness of our purpose."

"And what plan," cried the pretended shepherd, "can we form? I have already trod the intricate and dangerous road, and there is nothing better for us than to tread my footsteps back again. The day is particularly unfavourable, as it is accompanied with activity and business. We must therefore wait for the night. Then we must watch our opportunities, and embrace the favourable interval. Imogen, I feel not for myself. I do not throw away a thought upon my own safety, and I am ready to submit to every evil for your service and your defence. But yet, my gentle, noble-minded shepherdess, I cannot promise any very flattering probability of success. Indeed my hopes are not sanguine. The difficulties that are before us appear to me insurmountable. One mountain peeps through the breaches of another, and they are like a wall built by the hand of nature, and reaching to the skies. Penmaenmawr is heaped upon Snowdon, and Plinlimmon nods upon the summit of Penmaenmawr. It is only by the intervention of a miracle that we can ever revisit the dear, lamented fields of Clwyd. Let us then, my Imogen, compose ourselves to the sedateness of despair. Let us surrender the success of our future efforts to fate. And let us endeavor to solace the short and only certain interval that we yet can call our own, by the recollection of our virtuous loves."

"Alas," cried Imogen, "I understand not in what the sedateness of despair consists. In the prospect of every horrid mischief, mischief that threatens not merely my personal happiness or mortal existence, but which bears a malignant aspect upon the dignity of honour and the peace of integrity, I cannot calmly recollect our virtuous loves, or derive from that recollection sedateness and composure. Edwin, your language is dissonant, and the thoughts you seek to inspire, jarring and incompatible. If you must tell me to despair, at least point me to some nobler source of consolation, than the coldness of memory; at least let us prepare for the fate that awaits us in a manner decent, manly, and heroic."

"Yes, too amiable shepherdess, if I were worthy to advise, I would recommend a more generous source of consolation, and teach you to prepare for futurity in a manner worthy of the simplicity of your heart; and worthy of that disinterested affection we have ever borne to each other. Think of those sacred ties that have united us. Think of the soft and gentle commerce of mutual glances; the chaste and innocent communication with which we have so often beguiled the noontide hour; the intercourse of pleasures, of sentiments, of feelings that we have held; the mingling of the soul. Did not heaven design us for each other? Is not, by a long probation of simplicity and innocence, the possession of each other become a mutual purchase? An impious and arbitrary tyrant has torn us asunder. But do the Gods smile upon his hated purpose? Does he not rather act in opposition to their decrees, and in defiance of their authority?"

The magician paused. "Alas," replied the shepherdess, "what is it you mean? Whither would you lead me? I understand you not. These indeed were motives for fortitude and exertion, but what consolation can they impart to the desponding heart?" "I will tell you," replied her seducer, folding her slender waist with one of his arms as he spoke. "Since the Gods are on our side, since heaven and earth approve our honest attachment, let us sit here and laugh at the tyrant. While he doubles his guards, and employs all his vigilance, let us mock his impotent efforts."

"Ah," replied the shepherdess, her eye moistened with despair, and beaming with unapprehensiveness, "how strange and impracticable an advice do you suggest! Full of terror, full of despair, you bid me laugh at fear. Threatened by a tyrant whose power is irresistible, and whose arts you yourself assure me are not to be evaded, you would have me mock at those arts, and this dreaded power. Is not his power triumphant? Is not all his vigilance crowned with a fatal success? Are we not his miserable, trembling, death-expecting victims? Can we leave this apartment, can we almost move our hand, or utter our voice, for solicitude and terror? Oh Edwin, in what mould must that heart have been cast, what must be its hard and unsusceptible texture, that can laugh at sorrow, and be full of the sensations of joy, though surrounded with all the engines of wretchedness?"

"Imogen, your fears are too great, your anxieties exaggerate the indigence of our condition. Though we are prisoners, yet even the misfortunes of a prison have their compensations. The activity of the immaterial mind, will not indeed submit long without reluctance to confinement and restraint. But we have not yet experienced lassitude and disgust." "Alas, Edwin, how strange and foreign are thoughts like these! Whither do they tend? What would you infer from them?"

"This my love I would infer. That within one little cincture we are yet absolute. No prying eye can penetrate here. Of our words, of our actions, during a few remaining hours, we can dispose without controul."

"Ah," exclaimed the shepherdess, struck with a sudden suspicion of the treacherous purpose, and starting from her betrayer, "ah, Edwin, yet, yet explain yourself! A thousand horrid thoughts — a thousand dire and shapeless phantoms — But Edwin, — sure — is plain, and artless, and innocent. — What boots it that we can dispose of our words and actions within this cincture? — Will that enable us to escape? — No, no, no, no. — Escape you say is hopeless — What is it you mean? — Say — explain yourself — Oh, Edwin!" —

"Be not alarmed," cried the remorseless villain. "Listen, yet listen with calmness to the suggestions of my deliberate mind. Imogen, you are too beautiful — I have beheld you too long — I have admired you with too fierce an ardour. The Gods — the Gods have joined us. It is guilt and malignity alone that oppose their purpose. — Let us beat them down — trample them under our feet — employ worthily the moment that yet remains." —

As the magician pronounced these words, he advanced towards his captive, and endeavoured to seize her in his arms. But she thrust him from her with the warmest indignation; and contemplating him with an eye of infinite disdain, "Base unworthy swain!" — she cried — "Insidious traitor! — abhorred destroyer! — And is it thus that you would approach me? — Is it thus that you would creep into the weakness of my heart? — But fly — I know you not — One mark of compassion I will yet exhibit, which you little deserve — Fly — I will not deliver you into the hands of your rival, whom yet my soul does not so much loath and abhor — Fly — Live to be pointed at as an example of degeneracy — Live to blush for and repent of that crime, which, Edwin! — cannot be expiated."

Roderic had advanced too far to be thus deterred. He did not wish to manage the character under which he appeared. His passions by this interview, more private, and in which his captive had beheld him with an eye of greater complacency than ever, were inflamed to the extremest degree. The charms of Imogen had been in turn heightened with joy, and mellowed with distress. Even the conscious dignity, and haughty air she now assumed, gave new attractions to her form, and new grace to her manner. Her muscles trembled with horror and disdain. Her eloquent blood wrought distinctly in her veins, and spoke in a tone, not more dignified than enchanting. Her whole figure had a life, an expression, a loveliness, that it is impossible to conceive.

Roderic rushed forward unappalled, and unsubdued. He had already seized his unwilling victim. In vain she resisted his violence; in vain she strove to escape from her betrayer. "For pity's sake — for mercy's sake — for the sake of all our past endearments — spare me! — relent — and spare me — spare me! —" For a time she struggled; but her tender frame was soon overcome by the strength of her destroyer. She became cold and insensible in his arms.

At this moment a flood of splendid lightning filled the apartment. The air was rent with the hoarse and deafening roar of the thunder, the door flew open, and the form of that spectre that he most abhorred stood before Roderic. "Go on," cried the phantom, "complete thy heroic purpose. Scorn the tremendous sounds that now appal thee. They are but the prelude of that scene that shall shortly feast my eyes. Perceivest thou not the earth to tremble beneath thy feet? Hearest thou not the walls of thy hated mansion cracking to their ruin? Confusion is at hand. *Chaos is come again.* Go on then, Roderic. Complete thy heroic purpose." The spectre vanished, and all was uninterrupted silence.

The whole mind of Roderic was transformed from what it was. For the impotence of lust, and the cruelty of inexorable triumph, he felt the terrors of annihilation, and all the cold, damp tremblings of despair. But the victory of innocence was not yet complete.

Imogen had sunk for a moment under the horrors that threatened her, but she had not been so far impercipient as not to hear the murmuring of the thunder, and to see the gleam of the lightning. The form however that terrified Roderic, and the voice that addressed him, were perceived by him alone.

The shepherdess opened her eyes, and beheld the degenerate ravisher pale, aghast, and trembling. "It is well, Edwin. The Gods have declared themselves. The Gods have suspended their thunder over the head of the apostate. But, oh Edwin, could I have imagined it! Desolate and oppressed as I have been, could I have supposed, that that form was destined to fill up the measure of my woes! I once beheld it as the harbinger of happiness, as the temple of integrity and innocence. Oh, how wretched you have made me! How you have shaken all my most rooted opinions of the residence of virtue among mankind! Am I alone, and unsupported in her cause? How forlorn and solitary do I seem to myself! I suffered — once I suffered the thought of Edwin to mix with the love of rectitude, and the obedience of heaven. They all together confirmed me in the path I had chalked out for myself. Mistake not these reproaches for the weakness of returning passion. And yet, Edwin, though I loath, I pity you! Go, and repent! Go, and blot from the records of your memory the cold insinuation, the aggravated guilt that you have this day practised! Go, and let me never, never see you more!"

As she uttered these words, congratulation, reproach, wretchedness, abhorrence and pity succeeded each other in her countenance. But they were all accompanied with an ineffable dignity, and an angelic purity. The savage and the satyr might have beheld, and been awed into reverence. Roderic slunk away, guilty, mortified, and confounded. And such was the success of this other attempt upon the virtue of Imogen.

BOOK the SIXTH

IMOGEN ENDEAVOURS TO SUBDUE THE ATTENDANTS OF RODERIC.—THE
SUPPER OF THE HALL.—JOURNEY AND ARRIVAL OF EDWIN.—SUBTLETY
OF THE MAGICIAN.—HE IS DEFEATED.—END OF THE SECOND DAY.

THE magician, overwhelmed and confounded with uninterrupted disappointment, was now ready to give himself up to despair. "I have approached the
inflexible fair one," cried he, "by every avenue that leads to the female heart. And
what is the amount of the advantages I have gained? I tempted her with riches.
But riches she considered with disdain; they had nothing analogous to the temper
of her mind, and her uncultivated simplicity regarded them as superfluous and
cumbersome. I taught her to listen to the voice of flattery; I clothed it in all that
is plausible and insinuating; but to no purpose. She was still upon her guard; all
her suspicions were awake; and her integrity and her innocence were as vigilant as
ever. Incapable of effecting any thing under that form she had learned to detest,
I laid it aside. I assumed a form most prepossessing and most amiable in her eyes.
Surely if her breast had not been as cold as the snow that clothes the summit of
Snowdon; if her virtue had not been impregnable as the groves of Mona, a stratagem, omnipotent and impenetrable as this, must have succeeded. She beheld the
figure of him she loved, and this was calculated in a moment of distress to draw
forth all her softness. She beheld the person of him in whom she had been wont
to find all integrity, and place all confidence, and this might have induced her to
apprehend no danger. And yet with how much tender passion, with how distress-
ful an indignation, with what tumultuous sorrow did she witness his supposed
crime? What then must I do? What yet remains? I love her with a more frantic
and irresistible passion than ever. I cannot abstain from her. — I cannot dismiss
her. — I cannot forget her. Oh Imogen, too lovely, all-attractive Imogen, for you
I stand upon the very brink of fate! Nor is this all. Soon should I leap the gulph,
soon should forget every prudent and colder prospect in the tumult of my soul,
did not that cursed spectre ever shoot across my path to dash my transports, and
to mar my enjoyments. Which way shall I turn? To leave her, that is impossible.
To possess her by open force and manly violence, that my fate forbids. My understanding is bewildered, and my invention is lost. — Medoro!" —

Medoro received the well known signal, and stood before Roderic. He waited
not to be addressed, he read the purposes of the heart of the magician. "Roderic,"
cried he, "this moment is the crisis of you[r] destiny. The occasion, to which the
curse pronounced upon you by the inimical spectre refers, has already in part
taken place. YOU HAVE SUED TO A SIMPLE MAID, WHO BY YOUR CHARMS HAS BEEN
TAUGHT TO HATE THE SWAIN THAT ONCE SHE LOVED. It only remains that she should
persevere in the resistance she has hitherto made, and that A SIMPLE SWAIN, perhaps
her favoured Edwin, should defy your enchantments. Think then of the precipice
on which you stand. Yet, yet return, while it is in your power. One step in advance

beyond those you have already taken may be irretrievable. Alas, Roderic, it is thus that I advise! but I foresee that my advice will be neglected. The Gods permit to the invisible inhabitants of air, when strongly invoked by a mortal voice, to assist their vices and teach adroitness to their passions; but they do not permit an invocation like this to receive for its reward the lesson of moderation, and the attainment of happiness.

"Go on then, Roderic, in the path upon which you are inflexibly determined. You succeeded not in the stratagem of flattery; but it served to take off the keenness of the aversion of Imogen. She contemplates you now with somewhat less of horror, and with a virtuous and ingenuous fear of uncandidness and injustice upon your account. Neither have you succeeded in that deeper stratagem and less penetrable deceit, the assumption of the form of him she loved. It has however served to weaken her prepossessions, and relax the chains of her attachment. She is now the better prepared to receive openly and impartially the addresses of a stranger swain. Thus even your miscarriages have furthered your design. Thus may a wise general convert his defeats into the means of victory. Think not however again to approach her in the coolness of reason, and the sobriety of the judgment. Hope not by temptation, by flattery, by prejudice, to shake the immutable character of her mind. There is yet one way unessayed. You must advance, if you would form the slightest expectations of victory, by secret and invisible steps. Her virtue must be surrounded, entangled and enmeshed, or ever her suspicions be awakened, or her integrity alarmed. This can be effected only by the instrumentality of pleasure. Pleasure has risen triumphant over many a heart that riches could not conquer, and that ambition could not subdue. What though she has resisted temptation under the most alluring form, when her thoughts were collected and all around was silence? — Let the board of luxury be spread. Let the choicest dainties be heaped together in unbounded profusion. Let the most skilful musicians awake the softest instruments. Let neatness, and elegance, and beauty exhibit their proudest charms. Let every path that leads to delight, let every gratification that inebriates the soul be discovered. If at that moment temptation approach, even a meaner and less potent temptation may then succeed. The night advances with hasty feet. Night is the season of dissipation and luxury. Be this the hour of experiment, and let the apprehensive mind of Imogen be first assiduously lulled to repose. Here, Roderic, you must rest your remaining hopes. There is not another instrument can be discovered, to disarm and vanquish the human mind. If here you fail, the Gods have decreed it — they will be obeyed — Imogen must be dismissed from the enchanted halls of Rodogune."

With these words the goblin disappeared. The warning he had uttered passed unheeded, but the magician immediately prepared to employ this last of stratagems. Summoning the train of attendants of either sex that resided in the castle, he directed them some to make ready the intended feast, and some to repair to the apartment of Imogen. The preparations of the enchanted castle were not like those of a vulgar entertainment. Every thing was accelerated by invisible agents. The intervention of the retinue of Roderic was scarcely admitted. The most savoury viands, the most high flavoured ragouts, and the most delicious wines presented themselves spontaneously to the expecting attendant. The hall was illuminated with a thousand lustres that depended like stars from the concave roof, and were multiplied by the reflection of innumerable mirrors. The whole was arranged with inconceivable expedition.

In the mean time a few of the more distinguished attendants of her own sex repaired to the presence of Imogen. They found her feeble, spiritless and disconsolate. "Come," exclaimed their leader, in an accent of persuasion; "comply, my lovely girl, let not us alone have reason to complain of your unfriendliness and inflexibility."

Imogen was fatigued and she wished not for repose. Grief and persecution had in a former instance inspired her with the love of solitude. But her feelings were now of another kind. The disgrace and ingratitude of Edwin had wounded her in the tenderest point, and she could not think of it but with inexpressible anguish. She was for the first time afraid of her own reflections, and desirous to fly from herself. "Yes," exclaimed she, "and I would go, if you will promise me that it shall not be to the presence of Roderic. The castle and the fields, the freshness of the morning air and the gloom of a dungeon, are equal to me, provided I must be kept back from the arms of my beloved parents, and their anxious and tender spirits must still be held in suspence. But indeed I must not, I will not, be continually dragged to the presence of the man I hate. It is ungenerous, unreasonable, and indecent. What is the meaning of all this compulsion? Why am I kept here so much against my will? Why am I dragged from place to place, and from object to object? Surely all this cannot be mere caprice and tyranny. There must be in it some dark and guilty meaning that I cannot comprehend. Oh shepherdesses! if ye had any friendship, if any pity dwelt within your bosoms, ye would surely assist me to escape this hated confinement. Point but the way, show me but the smallest hole, by which I might get away to ease and liberty, and I would thank you a thousand times. You, who appear the leader of the throng, your brow is smooth, your eyes are gentle and serene, and the bloom of youth still dwells upon your face. Oh," added the apprehensive Imogen, and she threw herself upon her knees — "do not bely the stamp of benevolence and clemency that nature has planted there. Think if you had parents as I have, whose happiness, whose existence, are suspended upon mine, if you abbhorred, and detested, and feared your jailor as I do, what would be your feelings then, and how you would wish to be treated by a person in your situation. Grant me only the poor and scanty boon, that you would then conceive your right. Dismiss me, I intreat you. I cannot bear my situation. My former days have all been sunshine, my former companions have all been kindness. I have not been educated to encounter persecution, and misfortunes, and horrors. I cannot encounter them. I cannot survive it."

As she pronounced these words, she sunk, feeble, languid, and breathless, upon the knees of the attendant. They hastened to raise her. They soothed her ingenuous affliction, and assured her that she should not be intruded upon by him of whom she had formed so groundless apprehensions. Since then she was invited to partake of a slight refreshment accompanied only by persons of her own sex, she did not long hesitate, and was easily persuaded to acquiesce. The unostentatious kindness of the invitation, and the modesty of the entertainment she expected, dissipated her fears. It was from solitude that she now wished to escape; and it was to that simple and temperate relaxation that she had experienced among the inhabitants of Clwyd, to which she was desirous to repair.

She was conducted towards a saloon, which had less indeed of a sumptuous and royal appearance, but was more beautiful, more gay, more voluptuous, and more extatic than that which had been the scene of the temptation of the morning. The profuseness of the illuminations outdid the brightness of the meridian sun. The table was spread in a manner to engage the eye and allure the appetite. Every vessel that was placed upon it was of massive silver. And in different corners of the apartment heaps of the most fragrant incense were burning in urns of gold. The viands were of a nature the most stimulating and delicious; and the wines were bright and sparkling and gay. As Imogen approached, a stream of music burst upon her ear of a kind which hitherto she had never witnessed. It was not the sonorous and swelling notes of praise; it was not the enthusiastic rapture of the younger bards; it was not the elevated and celestial sounds that she had been used to hear from the lyre of Llewelyn. But if it was not so swelling and sublime, it was soft, and melodious, and insinuating, and overpowering beyond all conception. You could not listen to it without feeling all the strings of your frame relaxed, and the nobler powers of your soul lulled into a pleasing slumber. It was madness all. The ear that heard it could not cease to attend. The mind that listened to it was no longer master of itself.

Imogen entered the hall, and was received by a train of nymphs, some of them more beautiful than any she had yet seen, and all attired with every refinement of elegance and grace. Their hair was in part braided round their bright and polished foreheads, and in part it hung in wavy and careless ringlets about their slender necks, and heaving bosoms. Their forms were veiled in loose and flowing folds of silk of the finest texture, and whiter than the driven snow. The robes were not embroidered with gold and silver; they were not studded with emeralds and diamonds; but were adorned on every side with chaplets of the fairest and freshest flowers. Their heads were crowned with garlands of amaranth and roses. Though their conduct were tainted with lasciviousness, and their minds were full of looser thoughts, yet, awed by the virtuous dignity of Imogen, they suppressed the air of dissolute frolic, and taught by the guileful lessons of their lord, endeavoured to assume the manners of chaste and harmless joy.

The shepherdess, struck with the objects which so unexpectedly presented themselves to her eyes and her ears, started back with involuntary astonishment. "Is this," cried she, "the artless feast, and this the simple fare of which you invited me to partake?" "Imogen," replied the principal nymph, "we were willing to do you honour, and the preparation we have made is slight compared with that which the roof can afford. We considered your fatigue and your extraordinary abstinence, and we were willing to compensate them by pleasant food, and a grateful refreshment."

"And is such the grateful refreshment, and such the simple and unaffected relaxation that your minds suggested? Alas, were I to approach this board, it would be to me a business and not an amusement, an exertion and not a relief. A feast like this is an object foreign and unpleasing to my eyes. The feasts of the valley are chesnuts, and cheeses, and apples. Our drink is the water of the limpid brook, or the fair and foaming beverage that our flocks afford. Such are the enjoyments of sobriety; such are the gratifications of innocence. Virgins, I am not weary of the simplicity of the pastoral life. I hug it to my bosom closer, more fondly than ever."

"Amiable, spotless maiden! we admire your opinions, and we love your person. But virtue is not allied to rigour and austerity. Its boundaries are unconstrained, and graceful, and sweeping. It is a robe which sits easily on those who are formed to wear it. It gives no awkwardness to their manner, and puts no force upon their actions. Partake then, my Imogen, in those refreshments we have prepared for your gratification. If this be not duty, it is not crime. It is a venial and a harmless indulgence. Do not then mortify friends that have sought to please you, and refuse your attention to the assiduities we have demonstrated."

"No, my gentle shepherdess, it is in vain you plead. I would willingly qualify my refusal; but I must withdraw. The more you press me, the farther it is necessary for me to recede. In the morning of this very day, I was simple, and incautious, and complying. But now I have experienced so many wiles and escaped so many snares, that this heart, formerly so gentle and susceptible, is cased in triple steel. I can shut my eyes upon the most splendid attractions. I can turn a deaf ear to enticements the most alluring, and sounds the most insinuating. This is the lesson — I thank him for it — that your lord has taught me. You must not then detain me. I must be permitted to retire." And saying this she withdrew with trembling speed. In vain they insisted, in vain they pursued. Imogen escaped like a bird from the fowler, nor looked behind. Imogen was deaf to their expostulations, and indurate and callous as adamant to their persuasions.

The disappointment of Roderic, when he learned of this miscarriage of his great and final attempt was extreme. He coursed up and down the saloon with all the impatience of a wild boar pierced by the spear of the hunter, or a wolf from whom they have torn away her young. He vented his fury upon things inanimate. He tore his hair, and beat his breast, with tumultuous agony. He imprecated with a hoarse and furious voice a thousand curses upon those attendants who had permitted his captive to escape. Through the spacious hall, where every thing a moment before had worn the face of laboured gaiety and studied smiles, all was now desolation, and disquiet, and uproar. And urged as the magician had been by successive provocations, he was ready to overstep every limit he might once have respected, and to proceed to the most fatal extremities.

In this situation, and as Roderic was hastening with a determined resolution to follow to the apartment of Imogen, information was suddenly brought to him, that a young stranger, tall and graceful in his form, and of a frank and noble countenance, had by some unknown means penetrated beyond the precipices with which the enchanted castle was surrounded, and in spite of the resistance of the retinue of the magician had entered the mansion. The dark and guilty heart of Roderic immediately whispered him — "It is Edwin. — It is well. — I thank the Gods that they do not hold this aspiring soul in a long and dreary suspense! Let the destinies overtake me. I am prepared to receive them. Death, or any of the thousand ills that fortune stores for them she hates, could not come in a more welcome hour. — Oh Imogen, lovely, adorable Imogen, how vain has been my authority, how vain the space of my command! Let then my palaces tumble into ruin — Let that wand which once I boasted, shivered in a thousand fragments, be cast to all the winds of heaven! I will glory in desolation and forlornness. I will wrap myself in my poverty. I will retire to some horrid cave in the midst of the untamed desert, and shagged with horrid shades, that outgloom the blackness of the infernal regions. There I will ruminate upon my past felicity. There I will tell over enjoyments never to return. I will make myself a little universe, and a new and unheard of satisfaction in the darkness of my reflections, and the depth of my despair.

"And yet surely, surely the Gods have treated me severely, and measured out to me a hard and merciless fate. What are all the felicities I talk of, and have prized so much? Oh, they were seasoned, each of them, with a bitter infusion! Little, little indeed have I tasted of a pure and unmixed happiness. In my choicest delights, I have felt a vacancy. They have become irksome and tedious. I have fled from myself; I have fled from the magnificence of my retinue, to find variety. And yet how dearly am I to pay for a few gratifications which were in fact no better than specious allurements to destruction, and flowers that slightly covered the pit of ruin! In the bloom of manhood, in the full career of youth to be cast forth an UNPITED, NECESSITOUS, MISERABLE VAGABOND! All but this I could have borne without a sigh. Were I threatened with death, in this opening scene of life, I could submit with cheerfulness. But to drag along a protracted misery, to be shut out from hope, and yet ever awake to every cruel reflection and every bitter remorse — This is too much!"

From this dream of unmanly lamentations Roderic was with difficulty recovered by the assiduities of the attendants. At length incited by their expostulations to the collectedness of reflection and the fortitude of exertion, he determined, with that quickness of invention with which he had been endowed at his birth, upon a plan to elude, if possible, the perseverance of Edwin, and the menaces of his fate. Recollecting that his person was not unknown to the swain, he communicated his instructions to those who were about him, and withdraw himself into a private apartment.

It was Edwin. The instructions of the Druid of Elwy had relieved him from the insupportable burden that had begun to oppress his mind. Persuaded by him he had submitted to seek the refreshment of sleep. But sleep shed not her poppies upon his busy, anxious head. His mind was crouded with a thousand fearful phantoms. A child of the valley, he was a stranger to misfortune and misery. Upon the favoured sons of nature calamity makes her deepest impression, and an impression least capable of being erased. And yet Edwin was full of courage and adventure; he asked no larger boon than to be permitted to face his rival. But his inquietude was the offspring of love; and his wariness and caution originated in the docility of his mind, and his anxious attachment to innocence and spotless rectitude.

Having passed the watches of the night in uneasy and inexhaustible reflections, he sprung from his couch as soon as the first dawn of day proclaimed the approaching sun, and took a hasty leave of the hospitable hermit. Issuing from the grotto, he bent his steps, in obedience to the direction of Madoc, to that secret path, which had never before been discovered by any mortal unassisted by the goblins of the abyss. Before he reached it the golden sun had begun to decline from his meridian height. He passed along the winding way beneath the impending precipices, which formed a dark and sullen vault over his head. Ever and anon large pieces of stone, broken from their native mass, and tumbling among the craggy caverns, saluted his ear. Now and then he heard a bubbling fountain bursting from the rock, which presently fell with a loud and dashing noise along the declivity, and was lost in the pebbles below. The only light by which his steps were guided, was that which fell in partial and scanty streams through the fissures of the mountain, and served to discover little more than the shapelessness of the rocks, and the uncultivated horrors of the scene.

Through these Edwin passed unappalled. His heart was naturally firm and intrepid, and he now cased himself round with the armour of untainted innocence and unsullied truth. It was not long before he came forth from this scene of desolation to that beautiful and cultivated prospect which had already enchanted the heart of Imogen. To him it had advantages which in the former case it could not boast. He could contrast its gaiety and brightness with the obscure and dismal scene from which he had escaped. Nor was he struck only by the verdure of the prospect, and the vividness of its colours, he also beheld the inclosure, not, as his amiable mistress had done, from a terrace adjoining to the mansion; but from the last point of the rock from which he was ready to descend. The mansion therefore was his principal point of view from this situation. It stood upon a bold and upright brow that beetled over the plain below. The ascent was by a large and spacious flight of marble steps. Its architecture was grand, and simple, and commanding. It was supported by pillars of the Ionic order. They were constructed of ivory and jet, and their capitals were overlaid with the purest gold. An object like this to one who had never before seen any nobler edifice than a shepherd's cot, or the throne of turf upon which the bards were elevated at the feast of the Gods, was surprising, and admirable, and sublime in the highest degree.

"And this," exclaimed the gallant shepherd, "is the residence prepared for infamy and lust. The sun pours upon it his light with as large a hand, the herbage, the flowers and the fruits as fully partake of the bounteous care of nature, as the vales of simplicity and the fields of innocence. How venerable and alluring is the edifice I behold! Does not peace dwell within, and are not the hours of its possessor winged with happiness? Had my youth been spent among the beasts of the forests, had not my ears drank in the sacred instructions of the godlike Druids, I might have thought so. But, no. In vain in the extensive empire that the arts of sorcery and magic afford, shall felicity be sought. What avails all this splendour? and to what purpose this mighty profusion? All the possessions that I can boast, are my little flock, my wattled cottage, and my slender pipe. And yet I carol as jocound a lay, my heart is as light and frolic, and the tranquility of self-acquittal spreads her wings as wide over my bosom, as they could were I lord of a hundred hills, and called all the streamlets of the valley my own. The magician possesses a large hoard of beauty, and he can wander from fair to fair with unlimited and fearless licence. All merciful and benign beings, who dwell above this azure concave, give me my Imogen! Restore her safe and unhurt to these longing, faithful arms! Let not this arbitrary and imperious tyrant, who grasps wide the fairest productions of thy creation with a hundred hands, — let him not wrest from me my solitary lamb, — let him not seize for ever upon that companion, in whom the most expansive and romantic wishes of my heart had learned to be satisfied."

Such were the beautiful and virtuous sentiments of Edwin, as he beheld the empire of his rival from the head of the rock, and as he crossed the glade that still divided him from the object of all his exertions. From the eminence upon which he had paused for a few contemplative moments, the distance had appeared narrow and trifling. But the equal height of the ground upon which he stood, and of that which afforded a situation for the palaces of Roderic, had deceived him. When he looked towards the scene that was to form the termination of his journey, the glade below escaped from his sight. But when he descended to the plain, it was otherwise. One swell of the surface he had to traverse succeeded another; and the irregularity of the ground caused him sometimes to be lost, in a manner, in the length of the way, and took from him the consolation of being able so much as to perceive the object of his destination. As he passed the hills, and climbed each successive ascent, a murmur rose in his bosom; his impatience grew more and more ungovernable, and the eagerness of his pursuit taught him to imagine, that his little labour would never be done.

Every performance however of human exertion has its period; and Edwin had at length surmounted the greater part of the distance, and now gained a larger and more distinct view of the castle. But by this time the sun was ready to hide himself in the ocean, and his last rays now gleamed along the valley, and played in the party-coloured clouds. Meanwhile a dark spot, which had for some time blotted the brightness of the surrounding azure, expanded itself. The shades gathered, the light of the sun was hid, and the blackness of the night forestaled. The wind roared among the mountains, and its terrors were increased by the hollow bellowings of the beasts they harboured. The shower began; it descended with fury, and Edwin had scarcely time to gain the protection of an impervious thicket that crowned the lawn. Here he stood and ruminated. The solemnity of the scene accorded with the importance of his undertaking. The pause was friendly. He composed his understanding, and recollected the lessons of the hospitable hermit. He fortified himself in the habits of virtue; and, with a manly and conscious humility, recommended this crisis of his innocence to the protection of heaven.

The shower ceased, but the darkness continued. He had too well marked however the bent of his journey during the continuance of the day, to permit this to be any considerable obstacle. In the mean time it doubled and rendered more affecting the stilness of the night. Nothing was to be heard but the low whispers of the falling breeze, and the murmurs of the prowling wolf that now languished and died away upon the ear. This was the moment in which magic lords it supreme, in which the goblin breaks forth from his confinement, and ranges unlimited in the nether globe; and in which all that is regular and all that is beautiful give place to the hunger of the savage brute, and the witcheries of the sorcerer. But Roderic was otherwise engaged. His heart was employed in inventing guile, and was lulled into unapprehensive security. But Edwin was heroic. His bosom swelled with the most generous purposes; and he trusted unwaveringly in that guardianship that is every where present, and that eye that never slumbers.

He entered the walls of the enchanted castle. The novelty of the appearance of a stranger within the circle of those mountains, which no vulgar mortal had yet penetrated, the dignity of his appearance, and the boldness of his manner, at first distracted the attendants from the performance of that, which might have seemed most natural in their situation, and awed them into passiveness. He still wore that flowing and graceful garb, which was appropriated by the inhabitants of Clwyd to the celebration of public solemnities. He had passed through the midst of the shower, and yet one thread of his garment was not moistened with the impetuousness of its descent. His face wore a more beautiful and roseat glow than was native to its complexion. His eye was full of animation and expressiveness. Expectation, and hope, and dignity, and resolution had their entire effect in his appearance. "It is a celestial spirit!" cried they. "It is a messenger from the unseen regions!" and they sought in his person for the insignia that might confirm and establish their conjecture.

But such was not the imagination of Roderic. The master-guilt to which he was conscious, was ever ready to take the alarm upon any unexpected event; and he had immediately conjectured, by a kind of instinctive impression, who was this new and unwelcome guest. However unguarded and unprepared had been his retinue, they had recollected themselves sufficiently to detain Edwin in the avenue of the mansion, till they had received the orders of their lord. These were immediately communicated; and the magician withdrew himself till the proper period should arrive for his appearance to the swain.

Edwin, when he had entered the palace of Roderic, had been desirous, if it were possible, to push forward to the presence of his rival, without making any previous enquiries, or admitting of a moment's pause. The frequency however of the domestics had disappointed his purpose, and he was detained by them in spite of his efforts. "What means," cried he, "this violence? I must enter here. I will not be delayed. My purpose admits not of trifling and parley. To me every moment is big with fate." He said. For Edwin disdained the employment of falsehood and disguise. He lifted the javelin in his hand, but his heart was too full of gentleness and humanity rashly to employ the instrument of death. His tone however was resolute, and his gesture commanding, and the astonished attendants were uncertain in what manner to conduct themselves.

At this instant a domestic, who had received the instructions of his lord, entered the court. He had the appearance of superior dignity; and removing the attendants who pressed with rudeness upon the shepherd, he enquired of him the cause of his intrusion. "Lead me," cried Edwin, "to the lord of your mansion. My business is important and pressing, and will not admit of being communicated to any other ear. Whence this difficulty? Innocence does not withdraw from the observation of those who are desirous to approach it; and a manly courage is not apprehensive of an enemy."

"Young stranger," replied the domestic, "you are misinformed. This mansion knows not a lord. It belongs solely to proprietors of the softer sex, whom fortune has indulged as you perceive with every thing that is calculated to give new relish to the pursuits of life, and beguile the lazy foot of time. It is our boast and our honour to serve these damsels. And could my report add one ray to their lustre, I would tell you, that they are fair as the peep of the morning, and more fragrant than beds of violets and roses. It is their command, that humanity should be extended by all around them, not only to man, but to the humblest and weakest animals. Though you have entered their residence by mistake, we shall but fulfil the service they expect in furnishing you with every assistance and every accommodation in our power. If you are hungry, come in and partake of the liberal plenty the castle affords. If you thirst, we will cheerfully offer you the capacious goblet and the richest wines. If you are fatigued with the travel of the day, or have wandered from your path and are benighted in your journey, enter their mansion. The accommodations are large, and they are all free for the use of the poor, the necessitous, the unfortunate and the miserable."

Edwin listened with astonishment to the narration. He was not used to the address of falshood; and strongly warned as he had previously been of the iniquity of the train, the ingenuousness of his mind induced him at first without reflection to yield an easy credit to the story that was told him. It was related with fluency, plausibility, and gravity; and it was accompanied with a manner seemingly artless and humane, which it was scarcely possible for one unhackneyed in the stratagems of deceit to distrust and contradict.

"Surely," replied Edwin, "I cannot be wholly mistaken. At least has there not a young shepherdess just arrived here, tall, tender and beautiful, and whose flaxen tresses are more bright than gold, and more abundant than the blossoms in the spring?"

Before the officious domestic could reply to his enquiries, two of the nymphs, who had been attired for the feast of Imogen, came into the outer apartment in which the shepherd was, and advanced toward him. "These are my mistresses," cried the attendant. Edwin approached them with respect, and repeated his former enquiries. They were the most beautiful of the train of Roderic. They were clad in garments of the whitest silk, and profusely adorned with chaplets of flowers. Their appearance therefore was calculated to give them, in a shepherd's eye, an air of sweetness and simplicity that could not easily be resisted.

One of them was tall and majestic, and the other low, and of a shape and figure the most alluring. This appeared to be like a blossom in May, whose colours discovered to the attentive observer all their attractions, without being expanded to the careless eye: And that might be supposed to be a few summers farther advanced to a delicious maturity. The majesty of the one had nothing in it of the gross, the indelicate, and the forbidding; and the softness of the other was at-tempered with inexpressible propriety and grace. Both of them were gentle and affable. But the affability of the former took the name of benignity and conde-scension, and the affability of the latter was full of harmless gaiety, and a cheerful and unpretending spirit of society.

"We cannot," replied the elder, "attend to your enquiries here. The apartment is comfortless and inhospitable. You appear fatigued. And we pretend not, young stranger, merely to contribute what is in our power to relieve the uneasiness of your mind, we would also refresh your wearied frame. Come in then, and we will afford you every satisfaction we are able. Enter the mansion, and partake of the plenty the Gods have bestowed upon us, and which we desire not to engross to ourselves." During these words Edwin surveyed his fair entertainers with wonder and admiration. But enchanting as they were, they found not the avenue to his heart. There Imogen reigned alone, and could not admit of a rival. Even though upon a slighter occasion, and at less important moment, the purity of his mind, that virtue so much esteemed among the swains, could have been tainted, yet now that his undertaking whispered him, "Imogen alone is fair!" now that he feared for her safety, and hoped every moment to arrive at the dreaded, pleasing period of his anxiety, he could but be constant and be faithful. He recollected the sage instructions of the Druid of Elwy: and his resolutions were unshaken as the roots of Snowdon.

He accepted their invitation. Immediately, as upon a signal, an hundred flam-beaux lighted the area and lined the passage to the saloon of pleasure. The nymphs placed themselves on each side of the shepherd, and in this manner they passed along. If Imogen had been struck with the profuseness of the illumination, the richness of the plate, the sumptuousness of the viands and the wines, and the fra-grant clouds of incense that filled the apartment, how much more were they calcu-lated to astonish the soul of Edwin! He had comparatively passed through no pre-vious scenes; he had not been led on step by step; and the voluptuousness of the objects that now presented themselves before him had been unknown and unex-pected. The train of the subordinate attendants of the magician filled the apartment with beauty and with grace, and seemed to pay the most unreserved obedience to the nymphs that at first addressed him.

But before the shepherd had time to examine the objects that surrounded him, the musicians awaked their instruments, and all his faculties were engrossed with soft melody and enchanting sounds. The instrumental performance was illustrated and completed with a multitude of harmonious voices, and those who sang were each of them of the softer sex.

"What are the possessions most eagerly courted among mankind? Which are the divinities by mortals most assiduously adored? This goodly universe was in-tended for the seat of pleasure, unmixed pleasure. But a sportive, malicious divin-ity sent among men a gaudy phantom, an empty bubble, and called the shadow Honour. In pursuit of a fancied distinction and a sounding name, the children of the earth have deserted all that is bland and all that is delicious. Labour, naked, deformed, and offensive, they willingly embrace. They brave hardship and severity. They laugh at danger. From hence they derive the virtue of resolution, the merit of self-denial, and the excellence of mortification.

"But heaven did not open wide its hand, and scatter delight through every corner of the universe, without intending that they should be enjoyed. Enjoyment, indulgence, and felicity are not crimes. Abstinence, self-denial and mortification have only a specious mien and a fictitious merit. Did all mankind obey their fallacious dictates, the unlimited bounties of nature would become a burden to the earth, and fill it with pestilence and contagion. The soil would be oppressed with her own fertility; the herds would overmultitude their lords; and the crouded air would be darkened with the plumes of its numerous inhabitants. The very gems that now lie buried in the bosom of the ocean, would then bespangle its surface, and the dumb tenants of the watery tracts, inured to their blaze, would learn to leave the caverns of the sea and gaze upon the sun.

"Mortals, open your hearts to the divinity of pleasure! Why should he be in love with labour, who has a capacious hoard of choice delights within his reach? Why should we fly from a present good that we possess, to a future that we do not comprehend? Is this the praise we owe the bounteous Gods? Can neglect and indifference to their gifts be gratitude? This were to serve them like a timorous and trembling slave beneath the eye of an austere and capricious tyrant; and not with that generosity, that enthusiasm, that liberal self-confidence, which are worthy of a father, a patron and a friend.

"Ye that are wise, ye that are favoured of propitious heaven, drink deep of the cup of pleasure. The sun has now withdrawn his splendid lustre, and his flaring beams. The period of exercise is past, and the lids of prying curiosity is [are] closed. Night is the season of feast and the season of gaiety. In the graver hours of activity and industry, sobriety may be proper. It may then be fit to listen to the dictates of prudence, and pay some attention to the prejudices of mankind. The sternness of age and the austerity of censoriousness are now silent. Now pleasure wears a freer garb; and the manners of enjoyment are more frank and unrestrained. The thinness of indiscretion and the airy forms of inadvertence are lost and annihilated amid the shadows of the night.

"Now the numerous inhabitants of the waters come forth from their oozy beds and play and flounce in the beams of the moon. Round the luminary of the night the stars lead up the mystic dance, and compose the music of the spheres. The deities of the woods and the deities of the rivers come out from their secret haunts, and keep their pastimes unapprehensive of human intrusion. The elves and the fairies repair to their sports, and trip along the velvet green with many-twinkling feet. Let us imitate their amiable alacrity and their cheerful amusements.

"What has sleep to do with the secrecy and silence of the night? It is the hour of pleasure unrestrained and free. It is the hour in which the empire of beauty is complete, and those mysteries are disclosed which the profaner eye of day must never behold. Ye that are wise, ye that are favoured of propitious heaven, drink deep of the cup of pleasure! The festive board is spread before you; the flowing bowl is proffered for your acceptance. Beauty, the crown of enjoyment, the last perfection of society, is within your reach. Be wise and taste. Partake of the munificence the Gods vouchsafe."

As the song proceeded the two nymphs, who had first appeared to Edwin, and since attended him with the extremest officiousness, endeavoured by every artful blandishment to engage his attention, and rivet his partiality. They exerted themselves to suppress the grossness, inelegance and sensuality to which they had commonly been habituated, and to cover the looseness of the passions with the veil of simplicity, delicacy, and softness. As the music ceased, the master of the spectacle came forth from his retreat. But his figure was no longer that which bespoke the magician, and which Edwin had already seen. He appeared in the form of a youth of that age in which the frolic insignificance of childhood gives place to the eagerness, the enthusiasm and the engaging manners of blooming manhood. His habit was that of a cupbearer. His robes were of azure silk, and floated in graceful folds as he passed along. The beauty of his person was worthy of the synod of the Gods. His features had all the softness of woman without effeminacy; and in his eye there sat a lambent fire which bespoke the man, without roughness, and without ferocity. In one hand he bore a crystal goblet full of every potent enchantment, and which rendered him who drank for ever a slave to the most menial offices and the most wanton caprices of his seducer. In the other hand he held loosely, and as if it had been intended merely to give a completeness to his figure and a gracefulness to his step, that irresistible wand by which the majesty of man had often been degraded, and the reluctant spirit had been conjured up from the caverns of the abyss. The goblet he delivered to the elder nymph, who presented it, with inimitable grace and a bewitching condescension, to the gallant shepherd.

Edwin had the fortitude of a hero, but he had also the feelings of a man. He could not but be struck with the beauty of the nymphs, he could not but be surprised with the profuseness of the entertainment, and the richness of the preparations. The soul of Edwin was full of harmony. It had been one of his earliest and most ruling passions. No shepherd excelled him in the skill of the pipe, no shepherd with a sweeter or more sonorous voice could carol the rustic lay. Even the figure assumed by Roderic, his garb, his step, his gesture had something in them of angelic and celestial without the blaze of divinity, and without the awfulness that surrounds the godlike existencies, that sometimes condescend to visit this sublunary scene. The shepherd took into his hand the fatal bowl.

In the midst however of all that was attractive, and all that was unknown, Edwin had not forgotten the business that had brought him hither and the lessons of Madoc. The visage of Imogen, ever present to his soul, suggested these salutary reflections. By her assistance he strengthened all his resolutions, and gave vigour to the heroism of his mind. Through the memory of Imogen he derived a body, and communicated a visible form to the precepts of rectitude; and virtue wore all those charms that had the most uncontroled empire in his bosom. Half way to his lips he raised the cup of vice, and inexorable fate sat smiling on the brim. He paused; he hesitated. By an irresistible impulse of goodness he withdrew the fatal draught. He shed the noxious composition upon the ground, and hurled from him with indignation the vessel in which it had been contained.

Roderic beheld the scene with deep emotion, and was agitated by turns with a thousand passions. He saw the issue with confusion, despondence and fury. The roseat smiles of the cupbearer vanished; and, without the notice and consent of his mind, his limbs resumed their wonted form, and his features confirmed the suspicions of the shepherd, that he was now confronted with his mortal enemy. Thrice the magician invoked the spirit of his mother, and thrice he conjured the goblins, the most potent that ever mix in the mortal scene. He lifted the wand in his hand. It was the fiery ordeal that summons human character to the severest trial. It was the *judgment of God* in which the lots are devoutly committed to the disposal of heaven, and the enthroned Divinity, guided by his omniscience of the innocence of the brave, or the guilt of the presumptuous, points the barbed spear, and gives a triple edge to the shining steel. If the shepherd had one base and earth-born particle in his frame, if his soul confessed one sordid and sensual desire, now was the time in which for his prospects to be annihilated and his reputation blotted for ever, and the state and empire of his rival to be fixed beyond the power of human machinations to shake or subvert it. "Presumptuous swain!" cried the sorcerer, "what folly, what unmeaning rashness has brought you within the circle of my incantations? Know that from them no mortal has escaped; that by them every swain, whom adventurousness, ignorance, or stratagem has introduced within these limits, has been impelled to assume the savage form, and to herd with the most detestable of brutes. Let then thy foolhardiness pay the penalty which my voice has ever annexed to it. Hence to thy fellows! Go, and let their hated form bely the reason thou shalt still retain, and thy own voice affright thee, when thou shalt groan under irremediable misery!"

The incantation that had never yet failed of its hated purpose was pronounced in vain. Edwin had heard it unappalled. He wore the amulet of Madoc. He opposed to it the unconquered shield of spotless innocence. Even in the midst of the lordly despotism and the imperious haughtiness of his rival, he had been conscious to the triumph which nothing but the calmness of fortitude and the serenity of virtue can inspire. He was mindful of the precepts of the Druid. While Roderic was overwhelmed with disappointment and despair, he seized the wand of the magician, and with irresistible vigour wrenched it from his hand. He struck it with violence upon the ground, and it burst into a thousand shivers. The castle rocked over his head. Those caverns, which for revolving years had served to hide the iniquity and the cruelty of their possessor, disclosed their secret horrors. The whole stupendous pile seemed rushing to the ground. A flood of lightning streamed across the scene. A peal of thunder, deafening and tremendous, followed it. All now was vacancy. Not a trace of those costly scenes and that magnificent architecture remained. The heaven over-canopied the head of Edwin. The clouds were dissipated. The light of innumerable stars gave grandeur to the scene. And the silver moon communicated a milder lustre, and created a softer shade. Roderic and his train, full of pusillanimity and consternation, had fled from the direful scene, and vanished like shadows at the rising of the sun.

No mortal, but our lovers, had ever entered the enchanted mansion without having their characters disgraced, and their hearts thronged with all those hateful and dissolute passions, which distinguished the band of Roderic. No mortal was there, but our lovers, of the numerous inhabitants of this bad edifice, who had not shrunk from the earthquake and the solemnities that accompanied its subversion. Edwin and Imogen were alone. The shepherdess had listened to all the horrors of the scene with a gloomy kind of satisfaction. "What new wonders," cried she, "are now to be disclosed? What purpose are they intended to answer! The amendment, or the destruction of my betrayer? But it is well. Though the elements mix in inextricable confusion, though the earth be destroyed, yet has innocence no cause to fear. Alas, though I myself should be buried in the ruin, why should I apprehend, or why lament it? I was happy; untaintedly, uninterruptedly happy. But I am miserable. I am confined here in a loathsome, detested prison. Even my conduct is shut up with difficulties, and my bosom disquieted with the conflict of seeming duties. Even Edwin, the swain to whom my heart was united, and from whose memory my integrity derived new strength is corrupted, depraved and base. Let then destruction come. I will not lament the being cut off in the bloom of youth. I will not shed one tear, or feel one fond regret, but for the calamity and disappointment of my parents."

But however the despair of Imogen armed her courage against the concussions of nature, she yet felt that delicacy of constitution which characterises the most lovely of her sex, and that amiable timidity which often accompanies the most invincible fortitude. When the thunder roared with so fearful violence, when the mansion burst in ruins over her head, she stood, trembling and breathless, at the tumult around her. Her safety was the first object of the attention of Edwin; and when she recovered her recollection she found herself in the arms of her lover. "My fair one, my Imogen," cried he, "have I recovered you through so many obstacles, and in the midst of so numerous dangers? Oh, how must our affection, the purest, brightest, that ever lighted a human breast, be endeared by our mutual calamities! But virtue is ever triumphant, virtue is never deserted of the watchful care of heaven. My trials, my lovely shepherdess, have been feeble indeed, when compared with yours. Your integrity is unrivalled, and your innocence has surpassed all that the bards have sung in their immortal lays. Come then, oh, dearer, far dearer than ever to this constant heart, come to my arms! Let delay be banished. Let the veil of virgin bashfulness be laid aside. And let us repair together to the presence of your parents to ask an united blessing."

While Edwin thus poured forth the raptures of his heart, Imogen turned towards him a languid eye, full of soft and silent reproach. She retired from him with involuntary horror. "No, shepherd," cried she, and waved her hand with graceful indignation. "Like you I approve the justice of the Gods in the banishment of Roderic. But I think that justice would have been more complete, had it included in its vindictive appearance the punishment of the base, degenerate Edwin. Unworthy Edwin, to how vile and earth born sentiments has your heart been conscious! But go. Hence from my sight! The very spectacle of that form which I had learned to love is mildew and contagion to my eyes. Oh, Edwin, for your sake I will distrust every attractive form and every ingenuous appearance. The separation, my swain, is hard. The arts of Roderic came not near my soul, but your baseness has fixed an indelible wound. But think not — cherish not the fond mistake — that I will ever forget your ungenerousness in the hour of my distress and forlornness, or receive that serpent to my heart again."

As she pronounced these words, she hastened to fly from her imaginary enemy. Edwin detained her by a gentle violence. With much intreaty and a thousand soft blandishments, he wrung from her the story of her indignation. He related to her the tale of Madoc, and told her of the magic arts of his rival. He fully explained the scene of the pretended repentance of Roderic, and the seduction he had attempted to practise under the form of Edwin. As she listened to the wondrous story, Imogen trembled at the unknown dangers with which she had been environed, and admired more than ever the omnipotence of that virtue which had been able to lead her safely through them all. The conviction she received of the rectitude and fidelity of Edwin was to her, like the calm breath of zephyr, which succeeds the tremendous storm upon the surface of the ocean; and like that sovereign balm, which the sage Druids pour into the wounds of the shepherd, and restore him at once to salubrity and vigour. The amiable pair repaired with speed, and arrived with the dawn of the sun to the cottage of Imogen. At the sight of them the venerable Edith reared her drooping, desponding head, and the cheeks of the hoary father were bedewed with the tears of transport. Such were the trials of our lovers, and of correspondent worth was the reward they received. Long did they dwell together in the vale of Clwyd, with that simplicity and attachment which no scenes but those of pastoral life can know. Their happiness was more sensible than that of the swains around them in that they had known a reverse of fortune. And their virtue was the purer and the more benevolent, in that they had passed through the fields of trial; and that only through the ordeal of temptation, and an approved fortitude, they had arrived to the unmixed felicity, and the uninterrupted enjoyment they at length possessed.

THE END

Appendix: Critical Discussion

Felix Culpa

GODWIN'S *Imogen* was so little regarded by its author and his book-ish family that no copy survived even in their own libraries. It would be officious to point out faults in the work if it were not for the fact that the faults are extremely significant. There is good writing in the story, but the periodic and almost predictable appearances of "bad" writing make us grateful for a chance to see what William Godwin discarded as he moved toward *An Enquiry Concerning Political Justice* and *Things as They Are*. The romance stands in relation to his life work as *Comus* and *Rasselas* to the work of Milton and Johnson, and its faults arise from his not having found a myth in which he could believe. Milton believed in his magic wand, Johnson in his Happy Valley, but Godwin did not believe in the magic powers that supply the dynamics of his plot.

Yet he did believe in certain elements of the story. He urged men to look to the future, glancing back to the past only to observe and correct its errors, but even in *Political Justice* he stated a naive belief in a Golden Age. "Men associated at first for the sake of mutual assistance. They did not foresee that any restraint would be necessary to regulate the conduct of the individual members of the society towards each other or towards the whole. The necessity of restraint grew out of the errors and perversity of the few." The choice of the pastoral form, with its convention of an Age of Gold in ancient Britain, had a validity that can be felt in the opening scenes with their recognizable Welsh locale.

It is appropriate to his beliefs that he pictured the palace of evil not as a Gothic pile, but with features similar to the great houses of his day, neo-Greek with Ionian columns, with a garden that might have been laid out by Kent. It was conventional for the time that virtuous contentment should reside in a valley, evil be associated with mountainous regions, yet the imagistic settings are accomplished with a skill that calls to mind the system of imagery which throughout *Caleb Williams* connects inner turbulence with turbulence of the outer world. Rain, cold, storm are settings for spiritual distresses. Verbal images of avalanche, sunken river, whirlwind, precipice, and thunder reinforce the actual cataclysms. An early symptom of Falkland's mental turmoil was his strange desire to gaze upon mountains and crags.

Druids were in vogue, as Mr Marken has pointed out in his introduction. In 1787 General Conway added to his famous "wild" garden a small Druid temple, discovered on the Isle of Jersey and presented by the grateful islanders to their Governor. He erected it at Park-place near Henley, where it formed an agreeable adjunct to the carefully constructed subterranean passage, the rustic cottage, the lonely tomb, the antique ruins, and other appurtenances of the popular show place. Horace Walpole called the temple "Little Master Stonehenge." Godwin had no more idea than General Conway that the Age of Gold might be restored by his Druid artifact, yet the choice of this era served an important artistic purpose. It allowed him to deal with a society that stood in no necessary moral relation to the Christian era, that had no need to argue oppressive questions of original sin and predestination. He needed a vocabulary that excluded the vocabulary of Calvinism.

For Godwin, the diction of *Imogen* was an efficacious finger exercise for the diction of *Caleb Williams*. It is difficult to excise the vocabulary of a lifetime. Not only habit, but three other ancillary forces pulled him in the direction of Biblical diction: the plot is from Milton, much of the machinery is from Milton and Spenser, and both the ode and the pastoral had for generations felt the influence of the pastoral passages of the Bible in vocabulary, image and rhythm. In *Imogen*, one feels some sense of loss from the studied avoidance of so large a body of common imagery, but the effect in *Caleb Williams* is quite different. There, the rejection forms a source of positive energy. Diction — as Donald Davie has said (in *Purity of Diction in English Verse*) — can take on power from the words that try to thrust their way into a text and are being constantly fended off. The level of diction in *Caleb Williams* is characteristically flat, but the flatness is seething. When at last (in Chapter 40) a Biblical imprecation erupts into the text, it comes with the voice of despair and in the words used by the priests of Baal to call upon their non-existent god.

Judged only by a standard of literary accomplishment, no character portrayal in the earlier novel predicts the masterful interplay of character in *Caleb Williams*, where the author shows his deep perception of how the persecuted takes on the attributes of the persecutor in a terrible sequence of infection, from Tyrrel to Falkland to Caleb, and on and on to all those minor characters made wretched and dishonest by Caleb. The sequence leads to the statement that man is a monster, greater in his guilt and in his suffering than any demon Milton could imagine, and leads to the final confrontation of good and evil where Caleb is seen as tragically akin to Falkland. But Roderic, Falkland, and Caleb each perverts what should have been a virtue (love of beauty, honor, knowledge) into his downfall; Roderic loves and desires the same Imogen that Edwin loves, and can easily take on the form of his protagonist. When the good Edwin confronts the evil Roderic, there appears one of those "faults" which make the work into something much more than a piece of sterile eclectism reflecting random rays from the day in which it was written.

At this confrontation, Roderic (who represents "evil") holds a wand which had come to him from Rodogune, who was "in league with the powers of darkness," deeply skilled in those "flagitious arts, which have cast a gloom upon this mortal scene" (p 45–46). The wand was the means "by which the majesty of man had often been degraded" (p 103), and was the instrument that made effective the arrogance and "lordly despotism" of him who wielded it. It "points a barbed spear" (suggesting Ithuriel's) and is a "fiery ordeal" that gives "a triple edge to the shining steel" (suggesting Michael's sword); it is, indeed, in Godwin's italics, the "*judgment of God*" (p 104). Evil is armed with a weapon usually placed on the side of good. From the point of view of correctness, this ambiguity of associations may not be admirable, but the passage speaks in the true voice of a man getting ready to denounce law as the greatest social evil.

Plot and narrative technique do not compare favorably with the later works where Godwin took *flight* as the pattern of his plots and realism as his technique, but there is honesty in his fumbling. Over and over he sets up situations that depend on magic, only to forget what he started out to do. He postulates magic, but cannot make good use of it. He did believe in some connection between poetry and the health of the state; the singing contest demonstrates positively what is seen in negative form when the editor sends word to Caleb that he never paid anything at all for verse. But Godwin, unlike Milton, did not believe in the power of poetry to bring about any real effect; his magic songs do not have any power. Those draperies on the castle walls with their themes conveyed by magical prophesy are a fine idea, but Godwin can find no use for them in the plot. The magical temptations by luxury are too easily disposed of. He takes considerable care in setting up his magic garden — and then forgets all about it. The scene unaccountably shifts indoors, not by magic, not because of the storm, but because of the author's absentmindedness.

He borrows a fine goblin from the Sleeping Beauty, but neglects to give the creature any of the strong motivation of injured pride to be found in the original legend. When Richard Wagner put his sleeping beauty to rest, he believed in that myth. When Wagner launched Alberich on his goblin career, he gave him such motivation as diverts a modicum of sympathy to him from the Rhine-maidens who deride him. Roderic's female attendants have remnants of good in them; Spenser would have saved all those victims of black magic, but Godwin in cavalier fashion forgets all about them. By contrast, the minor characters in *Caleb Williams* belong to him. He does not forget them, but brings them back from the West Indies ten years later, gives them a niece who twenty-five years later carries on their ideas. In that plot everything is used; here, much is wasted.

The happy ending enforced by the genre could be viewed as a piece of cheap and easy optimism; it restates the two themes of the book, that innocence protects the innocent, that happiness is happier from tribulation and testing, and with discreet speed rings down the curtain. At least it does not say that good has any power to reform evil. But these themes are Milton's, and they are not backed by any belief in Godwin's mind. He never presented with conviction any character whose innocence saved him, nor any happiness made happier by testing. To be sure, he said that happiness was the aim of social order, but his masterpiece pictures a social order from which all hope of happiness is gone. Godwin believed in courage, but not in happiness. He was a deeply pessimistic man, and there is a devastating integrity in his faltering and floundering with a happy ending to be accomplished by some "amulet." His "ideal society" pictured here is as insubstantial as the Godwinian Pantisocracy that was to have flourished on the banks of the Susquehannah.

MARTHA WINBURN ENGLAND

Queens College

Primitivism in *Imogen*

IT WOULD BE not only regrettable but also remarkable for a work as ingenious as *Imogen* totally to disappear from view within a year after its publication, for over one hundred fifty years. In fact, it continued to have a wide appeal, at least in America; in 1804 the circulating-library catalogue of Caritat, a well known bookseller, speaks of its being popular because it "is of a chaste and virtuous tendency and will afford entertainment and instruction." [1] We might even speculate that it continued to exercise an influence, for one of the readers of the work in New York may well have been Edgar Allan Poe, during his 1830–31 sojourn at West Point or his 1837 trip to the city. There are striking similarities between "The Fall of the House of Usher" and Godwin's novel: the name of Roderic, the unbalanced figure of sensuality; the song sung in each of the castles just before disaster strikes the structure; [2] the appearance of a "most abhorred spectre" who has burst open a door to warn each Roderic of his doom (*Imogen* p 88); and above all the use and description of the lightning storm which utterly fells the houses of both Roderics. [3]

The last word of the note in Caritat's catalogue also reminds us of the consistently didactic tendency in Godwin's novels, even these three of 1783–84, turned out quickly for ready cash from his publisher. Godwin's philosophical mind could not fail to express his deep-rooted convictions even in his hackwork. The message of *Imogen* concerned the foremost intellectual issue of the age, which had been so cogently expressed by Rousseau, in his *Discourse on the Origin of Inequality*, namely, the problem whether man's happiness diminishes as his technology improves and his government becomes more complex. The preface to *Imogen* reflects contemporary interest in the whole question of primitivism, manifested in the current glorification of folklore, the enthusiasm for the spurious Ossianic poems, the keen interest in the published voyages to the new worlds of America and Polynesia, and

---

[1] See George G. Raddin's reprint of Louis Alexis Hocquet de Caritat's *An Early New York Library of Fiction* (New York 1940) 29. In *Hocquet Caritat and the Early New York Literary Scene* (Dover, NJ 1953) 30–34, Raddin indicates that this library of 30,000 volumes, reduced to 10,000, was subsequently operated by other owners, with "no view of it after 1810."

[2] "The Haunted Palace" in Poe's tale describes just such a valley as forms the setting of Godwin's novel. For the song deprecating honor in *Imogen*, see p 97–98.

[3] "The whole stupendous pile seemed rushing to the ground. A flood of lightning streamed across the scene. A peal of thunder, deafening and tremendous, followed it. All now was vacancy" (*Imogen* p 104). Edwin's use of a magic wand, of course, precipitates the downfall.

even the discovery of England's possibly indigenous primitives, at Stone-henge.[4]

More specifically *Imogen* indicates its author's intense concern with Rousseau's postulates concerning the degenerative tendency of mankind, as expressed in the Dijon prize essay. Godwin's intense respect for Rousseau as a thinker had been expressed by imitation, even earlier, in his *Sketches of History*[5] and by direct attribution in the Seminary pamphlet of 1783.[6] Later, in *Political Justice,* he acknowledged that the works of Rousseau had given him "stimulus" since 1781, a claim substantiated by the many citations in the work itself.[7] To be sure, major shifts in Godwin's views on the role of adversity in exposing if not shaping virtuous character and on the role of a developed culture in ensuring continuous progress, separated him sharply in 1793 from the primitivism of Rousseau, and it would be well for students of *Imogen* to bear this difference in mind.

In this early novel the period is obviously intended to be that stage designated by Rousseau in his essay as the youth of mankind, preceding agriculture — the latter being an accomplishment practiced only by the magician Roderic "through a wondrous art, as yet unknown in the plains of Albion" (p 61). It is a period before all government and organization save that of the family: "Of all the shepherds of the valley, there isn't one that claims dominion and command over another" (p 59). In this period, Godwin and Rousseau agree, men can speak and cooperate in temporary mutual undertakings, such as song and dance contests for the sake of public esteem (p 29–40), but in Rousseau this esteem is the first source of inequality.[8] The setting in the novel is idyllic, in its primitive simplicity of wants and equality of relations, in both of which there is also a slight similarity to the final state of *Political Justice* (II 546–554) as well as to the fancied state of natural abundance delineated in the *Enquiry Concerning the Principles of Morals* by David Hume, Godwin's much admired precursor (Section II Part 1). In

---

[4] At the time of the writing of *Imogen,* Godwin himself recorded the measurements of the stones at Stonehenge on a paper preserved in the Abinger manuscripts, consulted in microfilm at the Bodleian Library.

[5] *Sketches of History* (London 1784, written several years earlier), Sermon V, p 131–133. His account of the evolution of language, from sturdy simplicity to decadent rhetoric, follows Rousseau's in the *Emile,* trans Foxley (London 1911) 141–143, and praises the plain talk of a "state of nature."

[6] *An Account of the Seminary that will be opened on Monday, the Fourth Day of August at Epsom in Surrey* (London 1783) 4, 7, 19, 27, 36, 42, and 53.

[7] See the Index of *Political Justice,* I li, and the acknowledgment, with reservations, in the *Enquirer* of 1797, 106.

[8] *A Discourse on the Origin of Inequality,* trans G. D. H. Cole (London 1913) 197. This edition will hereafter be cited.

tribute to Godwin's intention to instruct, the reviewers of the day accepted the settings as anthropologically accurate: "Calculated to revive ideas of the days of pastoral purity and innocence" and "Abound[ing] with tender sentiments, pleasing description, and an innocent simplicity of manners." [9]

It is clear, in this vista of ancient Wales, that Godwin is favoring a golden age preceding culture, as constituting the acme of felicity. It is a time devoid of excesses, for the Druids praise temperance (p 65); of cruelty (p 25); and of insincerity, save that introduced by the melodramatic villain, the wizard manipulator of property. Simplicity is eulogized repeatedly (p 44, p 50–51, p 106). The natural passions, source of anti-rational behavior in *Political Justice*, are said to be benevolent, especially in woman. The fair sex is given, as in Godwin's novels after *Caleb Williams*, the quintessential role of exhibiting the truest examples of "disinterested rectitude" as well as the most "penetrating wit," in contrast with "the strong, slow reason, the deep unfathomed science, and the grave and solemn wisdom" of man (p 68). Hints of the sources of the decline of future society are given in the misused learning and the misapplied private possessions of Roderic, just as in Rousseau — who advocated the banishment of printing, "a dreadful art" productive of "frightful disorders" (*Discourse* p 140). It should be remembered, of course, that Rousseau did not glorify the infancy of the race over the period which presupposes the development of language, tools, a limited degree of personal property, and a patriarchal and communistic social organization, a period "keeping a just mean between the indolence of the primitive state and the petulant activity of our egoism." The steps of man away from this condition, now found among savages, have been "toward the decrepitude of the species" (198–199) Rousseau asserts, rather illogically in view of his prefatory warning that this happy state perhaps never did exist (155). In both *Imogen* and Rousseau's essay it was not government *per se* which introduced dissension and misery into the idyllic pastoral state, but rather an ambition to enjoy products requiring "the joint labour of several hands," leading to inequality through large scale private property, especially in the cultivation of metallurgy and agriculture (*Discourse* p 199–200). Roderic's palace of false pleasure has ceilings, capitals, and furniture of gold and is surrounded by "a rich scene of vegetable gold" (p 61), tended by "crouds of degenerate shepherds" (p 46); these also serve the voluptuous feasts in a capacity of subservience, which Godwin fifteen years later speaking of English servants calls "slavery" with "mitigations." [10] Even warfare is alien

[9] *The English Review* IV (Aug 1784) 142 and *The Critical Review* LVIII (Oct 1784) 312.
[10] *The Enquirer* (London 1797) 211.

to this pastoral life (p 44), and in *Political Justice* it was to be warfare which provoked Godwin's strongest indictment of "political society" (*PJ* I 7–8). Godwin's condemnation of the division of labor, paralleling that in Rousseau, was always a note in his later writings, since he regarded most modern technological advances as primarily instruments of further exploitation or methods of producing quite useless or even harmful superfluities.[11] Yet he was quite consistently capable of praising automatic machinery which would almost totally relieve all mankind of manual or stultifying labor.[12]

Imogen presents another theme dear to the disputants over primitivism, the relative advantages of the primitive state over those of a state which permits the testing of virtue by adversity. For the purpose of motivating his tale, Godwin does speak of the virtue of Imogen and Edwin as "the purer and the more benevolent, in that they had passed through the fields of trial" (p 106). The contrast, however, between vice and virtue, good and evil, is not basic to the tendency of the story itself, since it is largely an intuitive goodness which protects the heroine, as in *Comus*. "Happiness in this sublunary state can scarcely be felt, but by a comparison with misery" (p 50), is a statement applying to the satiety of the over-indulged Roderic, not to the "envied simplicity — venerable ignorance — plenteous poverty" of the shepherds. Despite his Socratic emphasis upon virtue through knowledge ten years later, in *Political Justice*, Godwin specifically then tries to exempt humanity from the need for participating in diametrically opposed experiences in order to make correct choices. "It is no more reasonable to suppose that virtue cannot be matured without injustice, than to believe . . . that human happiness cannot be secured without imposture and deceit," he asserts (*PJ* II 7–8). His position in *Imogen* is basically no different, although the dramatic confrontation of innate virtue with powerful injustice, enforced with a Mephistophelean range of temptations, constitutes a standard, didactic plot far older than that of *Pamela*.

The goodness of Imogen is not totally intuitive, however; for Godwin, fresh from considering the ideal environment that his proposed seminary was to provide for a select group of children, allows for the humanizing effects of the perfect, shepherd existence. In the role of a modern utilitarian Roderic tempts her with a knowledge intended "to enlarge our sphere of sensation and to extend the sources of happiness" (p 65), a knowledge, he adds, which will make her more "generous and benevolent" to parents and

---

[11] *Political Justice* II 437 and 514; cf *Imogen* p 50 for the sensual refinements of Roderic.
[12] *Political Justice* II 503 and *Thoughts on Man* (London 1831) 199.

friends. Imogen's answer relies on the far from primitive exaltation of the mind, that "nobler part." Roderic then judges her to be "too well fortified with the prejudices of education and the principles of an imaginary virtue to be reduced by an assault" through knowledge. Since even his direct enticements of her senses fail, we can assume that "Mens sana in sano corpore [politico]" will still prevail over the beguiling landowners and enslavers of mankind. Symbolically, Roderic aims to curtail the equality and freedom of mankind in this Celtic utopia, and symbolically he is defeated, as he will be after the French Revolution, by a combination of "innate dignity and omnipotence in virtue" (p 83), and of the pursuit of "unblemished truth" (p 45), and "benevolence and justice" (p 60). These rather discrete elements can "burst forth again more illustrious than ever," after the fall of the house of Roderic (p 83), in the dawn of humanity and in the "dawn" of 1789. In a sense, therefore, one of Godwin's earliest novels is a prelude to his solid contribution as a renowned novelist and thinker and indicates the important but equivocal role which cultural primitivism played in his works.

BURTON R. POLLIN

The City College

Some Implications of Irony

AT THE RISK of reading more into *Imogen* than it may in fact contain, we may supplement the earlier discussions of this work by reconsidering the tone of Godwin's Preface. Dr Marken noted in passing that the Preface, with its calculated obfuscation, seems to have been purposely designed to expose the inattention or critical ineptitude of the superficial reader. The Preface first states that *Imogen* is the work of an Ancient, a translation from the Welsh of the bard Cadwallo; and then that it belongs to Rice ap Thomas, who is palmed off as a Modern, a contemporary of King William III (1650–1702). But Thomas, reports Dr Marken, really lived from 1449 to 1526. If Godwin was indeed sifting his audience by equivocation, we should certainly like to know how far and how deep his equivocation extends, or what uses it serves as a rhetorical instrument. It enables Godwin at the outset to reaffirm Dr Johnson's view that the poems of Ossian are spurious, modern works. Having assured us that the case for Cadwallo's authorship of *Imogen* is as secure as the case for the antiquity of "the celebrated Poems of Ossian" (p 21), the speaker soon rejects the hypothesis that *Imogen* is an ancient work, and hence it becomes the forgery of a Modern. The reader is left to draw his own conclusions about the authenticity of Ossian.

As the Preface continues, we learn that the "translator" of Rice ap Thomas's pastoral romance is also one of Thomas's descendents. Thomas himself seems to have preferred Cadwallo to all other Welsh bards, and often quoted from his *own* pastoral romance as proof of the greatness of Cadwallo! The "translator" sadly admits that he does not know "how to excuse this piece of jockeyship and ill faith, even in Rice ap Thomas . . . " (p 22). Godwin is clearly enjoying this parody of Macpherson, the "translator" of Ossian; but the Preface gives us more than simply this parody. It tells us how to take *Imogen*, by implying that this work may not be, after all, a straightforward pastoral romance. It becomes a different thing, perhaps in part a mock-pastoral, if we choose to believe that Godwin borrowed the technique of the mask or persona from, say, Swift's *Tale of a Tub*. As in that work, with its purposeful separation of Swift from the Grubean narrator and his tale, so do we find in the Preface to *Imogen* a somewhat unhinged or confused narrator who is a living descendent and "translator" of a somewhat unhinged and "humourous" Modern named Rice ap Thomas, a man who "abounded in singularities" (p 22). The "translator" further informs us that he himself, because of his own admiration for Milton's *Comus*, may very well have been responsible for the obvious "coincidencies" (verbal plunder from *Comus*) in the pastoral romance.

In view of this delightful eccentricity, ought we to continue reading *Imogen* as entirely a *bona fide* pastoral? If we do so we may have to accuse Godwin of being a serious bungler in the pastoral vein. The capricious, arbitrary, and sometimes absurd character of the plot can easily lead a critic to assert that this piece is mere hackwork, replete with "bad" writing from cover to cover. But Godwin may have been less of a hack at twenty-eight than some have imagined. It would be helpful to know which came first — the romance proper? or the satirical Preface with its hints of extended equivocation in the entire work? Was the Preface an afterthought by which the author could excuse a mediocre if not ridiculous pastiche of pastoral and romance motifs? Or is this erratic patchwork to be read as a parody of itself and of the general taste for tales redolent of cultural and chronological primitivism? *Imogen* is not a work of concentrated irony throughout, but critical discussion of what Godwin believed or did not believe in his story — its magical machinery, its divine supervision of virtue, its Happy Valley and related primitivistic thought — is rendered more difficult by virtue of this whimsical Preface. Its ironic tone inevitably makes us suspect the fiction that follows. At various levels the romance itself seems to parody the "translations" and "discoveries" of ancient manuscripts by Macpherson and Chatterton, the strong current taste for native bards and literary antiquities, and various stereotypes in the pastoral tradition. And yet we are irresistibly led to admit that Godwin's love of Milton and *Comus* is genuine, and that Milton's faith in the refining of virtue by opposition or adversity is eloquently restated in *Imogen*.[1]

A further line of irony which reviewers, then and now, have bypassed, provides specific support for the view that the Preface subtly complicates our attitude toward the romance. When the "translator" informs us that "It is impossible to discover in any part of it [this pastoral romance] the slightest trace of Christianity" (p 21), we are in no position to appreciate the complexity of this statement. It means simply that the story takes place in pre-

---

[1] According to Dr Martha W. England (above, p 112) "the two themes of the book, that innocence protects the innocent [and] that happiness is happier than tribulation and testing" . . . "are not backed by any belief in Godwin's mind." Perhaps her assumption is that true conviction or belief would inevitably or most likely have produced a work of greater artistic integrity. In view of the contempt with which informed opinion then regarded any serious use of supernatural machinery in a modern work, Godwin's apparent lack of faith in his own machinery is readily understandable. But didactic morality was generally encouraged, and Godwin may have been aiming both to please by parody and to instruct with impassioned rhetoric.

Christian Wales. But when we return to these words after having read all or even most of the romance, we cannot help being struck by the force of Godwin's irony, for some of the highest ideals of Christian ethics are certainly embodied in Edwin and Imogen. Another passage, that in which the hoary bard Llewelyn recites a quasi-Lucretian myth of the creation at the "religious" festival of Ruthyn (p 39), presents one of the eighteenth century's most popular alternatives to the corruptions of Christianity, namely, the natural religion imputed to all primitive peoples. Llewelyn sings out his version of "The Heavens declare the Glory of God" and is interestingly pre-Christian in his doctrine of rewards and punishments in the afterlife. Godwin may well be offering the pure, natural religion of the Druids as the preferable alternative to modern Christianity, a view suggested or implied in Toland's writings on the Druids. If so, then Godwin at this stage in his career reveals a sympathetic and partisan attitude toward deistic natural religion. Much of this is related to Dr Pollin's discussion of primitivism in *Imogen*, and further documents, it may be, the progressive deterioration of Godwin's religious faith in the 1780s. He later wrote that he "was not a complete unbeliever till 1787."

The view that the early 1780s were for Godwin years of intellectual indecision and transition seems to be suggestively if not empirically accurate, and *Imogen* may well be a faithful reflection of Godwin's wavering convictions at that time. If his pastoral is tentative and uncertain, so also is his irony. *Imogen* as a pastoral romance does not come off because Godwin's literary world valued realism in the novel and regarded pastoral make-believe as "exploded." It is not sufficiently a mock-pastoral because that same literary consensus had come to appreciate the noble simplicity of the primitive life; the mock-pastoral successes of John Gay were no longer the height of literary fashion. Probing further the limitations of *Imogen*, we find that Godwin is too often hampered by literary theory, or by his awareness of the requirements of an anachronistic or dispossessed genre. His literary self-consciousness is all too apparent, for instance, where he seems to be determining the character of pastoral:

> Imogen, though loved and honoured by the borderers of Towey, had
> been little used to studied commendation and laboured applause. Pastoral
> simplicity does not deal in these; and though it seek to oblige, its endeav-
> ours are unostentatious and silent. (p 70)

And when, continuing this passage, we learn that Imogen's "reverence for song was radical and deep" and that "from earliest infancy she had considered poetry as the vehicle of divine and eternal truth," we are presented with a theory of poetry, the inspiration theory, which Godwin's early literary effort totally belies. It is one thing to believe earnestly in the invincibility, the noble simplicity, and the enchanting beauty of Virtue; it is quite another, and more difficult matter, to enshrine this belief in immortal fiction. On the other hand, we have fortunately retrieved a preliminary formulation of the moral idealism of *Political Justice*, and can again observe how various and eclectic are the traditions he strove to unify. History did not deal unfairly with Godwin in having consigned *Imogen* to temporary oblivion. If we have not exhumed a masterpiece, we have at least recovered a work that can pleasantly exercise and stimulate our historical imagination.

IRWIN PRIMER

Rutgers-Newark College